Mudrooroo was born in Narrogin in Western Australia in 1938. He travelled extensively throughout Australia and the world and lived in Nepal for ten years, then spent the last ten years of his life in Brisbane. He died on January 14 2020. Mudrooroo had been active in Aboriginal cultural affairs, was a Member of the Aboriginal Arts Unit committee of the Australia Council, and a co-founder with Jack Davis of the Aboriginal Writers, Oral Literature and Dramatists Association. He piloted Aboriginal literature courses at Murdoch University, the University of Queensland, the University of the Northern Territory and Bond University. Mudrooroo was a prolific writer of poetry and prose and is best known for his novels, *Wildcat Falling* and *Master of the Ghost Dreaming;* and his critical work, *Writing from the Fringe. Old Fellow Poems* and *Wildcat Falling* are both available with his audio presentation. His last books were the novel *Balga Boy Jackson* in 2017, and the first volume of his memoirs, *Tripping with Jenny* in 2020.

Books by Mudrooroo available in ETT Imprint

Tripping with Jenny
Balga Boy Jackson
Wildcat Falling (ebook)
Doin' Wildcat
Wildcat Screaming (ebook)
Dr Wooreddy's Prescription for Enduring
   the Ending of the World
Long Live Sandawarra
The Indigenous Literature of Australia
The Garden of Gethsemane
An Indecent Obsession (ebook)
Aboriginal Mythology
The Kwinkan (ebook)
The Secret of Hanging Rock
Old Fellow Poems (ebook)
An Indecent Obsession (ebook)

Master of the Ghost Dreaming series:
Bk 1: The Master of the Ghost Dreaming
Bk 2: The Undying
Bk 3: Underground
Bk 4: The Promised Land

THE PROMISED LAND

Mudrooroo

ETT IMPRINT

Exile Bay

This edition published by ETT Imprint, Exile Bay 2021

First published by Angus & Robertson 2000
First electronic edition ETT Imprint 2017

ETT IMPRINT

PO Box R1906

Royal Exchange NSW 1225 Australia

ISBN 978-1-925706-01-7 (ebook)
ISBN 978-1-922473-64-6 (pback)

Cover: *The King of Terrors* by S.T. Gill
(State Library of New South Wales)

Cover design by Tom Thompson

In memory of Heiner Muller (1929-1996)

To keep writing as long as possible, without hope or despair.

'Allegorical,' she said, her voice raw, sounding as if she smoked and drank heavily, awaiting exit from the womb.
'Truth bedecked in Halloween drag.'

Jack Womack

CHAPTER ONE

Lady Lucille, or as she was affectionately known to her intimates, Lucy, since becoming a woman had been subjected to noctambulism. It was a pathological condition she bore sometimes well but often badly, as did her family and friends, who were afraid that this predilection (for they refused to look upon it as a sickness) might lead to the loss of her reputation and thus her marital prospects. A young girl roaming the streets in a somnolent state clad in flimsy night attire, they could see only as a gross indecency which must be checked and banished. 'It's a trial not to be accepted,' her mother complained to her father. After due conference, they called upon her best girl chum, Mina, who was level headed and might alleviate the condition by her presence. Mina came to share Lucy's chamber and bed, clasping the girl to her bosom as they slept. Alas, such precautions, though pleasurable, proved inadequate and in the early hours of a morning, Mina awoke to find her arms empty.

At the time, they had been staying in a picturesque fishing town in North Riding dominated by the ruins of an ancient abbey, below which was a cemetery with graves that were on the verge of slipping into the ocean. The combination of hilltop ruins, the ancient cemetery and the cliff edge had held them with its Gothic splendour. Such a romantic, though eerie, spot had stirred in the girls longings which they had discussed as they sat on their favourite mossy stone bench gazing over the port with its fishing vessels snugly safe from the windswept sea. They had talked of their future prospects and even of ghostly visitations as they eyed the eruption of another storm at sea. The indented coast was subject to sudden tempests; flashes of lightning and thunder had struck out above becalmed waters which then surged under a wind of gale strength and sheets of icy rain, from which the girls had had to flee like two startled birds.

Lucy had been languishing in the quiet town and needed to be fussed over. Sometimes she shivered as if from the cold, but complained that the constant flow and clash of the elements produced a magnetism that affected her emotionally. She confided in her friend that sometimes her innermost being was so infused that she had to rise and glide out into the open night air so that she might feel the electricity caressing her all over. 'Like a lot of little fingers rubbing away at my sensitive places, and right under my dress too,' she had said with a giggle to Mina, who reported the conversation to her chum's parents. They had all agreed that she was a weird little lass, who threatened them with continuing maintenance if she could not be settled. What had to be done was to get her a husband who would put a stop to all such flights of fancy; but where to find such a man? They had sighed and passed on their responsibility to Mina, whose arms, alas, relaxed in repose. The night had begun with a sudden rush of wind, though this time, instead of the crying of the heavens, there came a stillness with the electrical display above the moaning sea. Mina had drawn the curtains against the aerial disturbance. She had snuggled up against her friend, comparing breasts for some time, then finally drifted off, tightly holding on to the warm body beside her. The night light which was always kept burning had illuminated both their sleeping innocent faces.

Mina awoke to an ominous stillness. She tried to snuggle up to the remembered warmth and felt only the cold sheet. She rubbed her eyes and leaped out of bed, quickly pulling on a thick robe. Now her alarmed gaze fell on Lucy's dressing gown and day clothes. 'Poor dear thing,' she murmured. She snatched up her chum's gown, rushed downstairs, slipped the latch on the door and darted out into the darkness of the early morning. Heavy clouds were racing across the sky like thick strands of hair, but at ground level the air was motionless and weighed down as if by some fluidic pressure. Thankfully, the moon began glimmering through the thick strands to light her way. She dashed towards the cemetery and as she reached it saw on their favourite bench a sprawled female body draped in white.

'Lucy,' she whispered, then her eyes widened and, with an involuntary cry, she darted forward. A dark figure appeared to be embracing her chum.

But when she reached the bench, Lucy was alone. A trick of the light, Mina thought, as she gently shook the girl into some semblance of consciousness, wrapped the robe about her shivering form and led her back to the safety of their bed where she held Lucy's slight body and gently used her fingers to ease the trembling. With a slight moan, the girl pushed her hand aside and turned away and into sleep.

Fully alert, cheerful and even playful like a fluffy kitten in the full light of the morning, Lucy smilingly declared that she had no recollection of her nocturnal stroll, though she did admit to having had some dream in which a pair of red gleaming eyes had drawn her into a sweet phantasy, the details of which she blushingly declined to reveal. She levelled a meaningful glance at Mina who did not press her further, but who, with a stern sense of duty, informed her chum's parents of their daughter's latest escapade. They had not been able to keep hidden Lucy's sleepwalking and mood swings, and hence there was a dearth of eligible suitors. But their family doctor had advised them that, with all the duties and obligations of matrimony, women had little time to indulge in such nonsense: 'It is but the fluid intensity of a young woman's imagination, perhaps stirred by an unhealthy indulgence in the reading of narrative fiction, which will be unable to claim her when there is a husband to be attended to, especially in those conjugal rites which, although there is doubt on this matter, a young woman such as your daughter needs if she is to free herself of the neuralgic symptoms she is manifesting.'

Thus advised, they removed to Bath for Lucy to take the healing waters while they kept an eye out for a suitor of some means, preferably a mature man who would be able to give the necessary stability to their overimaginative daughter. It was on their second evening at the dinner table that the newly-titled knight, Sir George Augustus, made their acquaintance. Enquiries revealed that he was of dubious ancestry, though possibly of the Durham Augustuses, and a widower of independent means as well as of some status in scientific circles. Apart from this, he was short and rotund, with a baldness concealed by a wig of gingerish colour. He also had a roving eye and often it settled on Lucy. The parents did not object and they invited him to share their table. It was soon obvious that he was smitten by the pale, blonde girl and in proof of this he composed some indifferent verses:

> The sky's blue is bordered,
> Alack a daisy,
> By the fringed lashes of palest bronze;
> Let it be said that a beating heart
> Becomes all mazy
> With thoughts of sweet bindings,
> One to another.

This did elicit a smile from Lucy and, thus emboldened, he approached her parents, who, after ahumming and ahemming and a settlement of two hundred a year, agreed to him as a protector for their dear, dear daughter. He did not notice their sigh of relief. Lucy lurched into a crisis when she was presented with the decision. She wanted a young Byron (without the pain), not an ancient chap who, once when he had been seen walking with her, had become a laughing stock as a sudden dash of breeze had whipped the red wig from his head and sent it flying off like some errant rooster with him in short-breathed pursuit. Still, her parents made some allusion to her malady and to the necessary stability that a mature personage would engender on her flighty nature, and even sat genially through a tantrum or two as their daughter adjusted to the idea of her new future. Eventually, her sullen face creased with frown lines, Lucy surrendered her life. She found herself the wife of an elderly man, though one who did not neglect his marital duties and in his way loved her to some length; for, like many older men, he was slow to spend but he remained smitten, enjoying showing her off as a property well worth the expense.

Marriage did indeed put an end to her sleepwalking, but not to her dreams, which now were tinged with a vague eroticism which her husband's embraces stirred rather than alleviated. She turned pensive, restless with inchoate desires which fluttered her heart and pinched her face. She might have continued like this, growing steadily sour, had not Sir George received a commission to voyage to a faraway colony on a tour of inspection. This news raised her spirits and she twirled about the floor in a dance step. Of course she would be going, and where to? The Great South Land! It would be a perfect romantic wonderland, she knew it, she knew it. And Sir George, in the face of such enthusiasm, could not deny her the imagined pleasure, though he knew the substantiality was nowhere near the perfection of her dream.

At first glance, the Great South Land did seem romantic in its desolation; and before this impression could be replaced by one of tedious boredom, the young wife met a mysterious woman, a Mrs Amelia Fraser, who fascinated her much as a serpent is said to fascinate its prey. Lucy welcomed this feeling, for she had been pining for her best friend, Mina, now thousands of miles away in the motherland. The woman had a strange malady (that is, if it was not mere vanity) being unable to receive the full light of the sun on her skin. She appeared in public completely draped in black so that not a patch of pale skin showed. Even her features were hidden, beneath a deep bonnet and a closely woven net, Lucy had a somewhat unorthodox imagination and so Mrs Fraser became the dark figure to which she had surrendered in many of her dreams. Now, here she was in the flesh and just as powerful. Lucy's eyes sought to penetrate the veil and she flushed as she felt a return gaze examining her form. Her innermost being began to tremble with an intensity such as had left her gasping in the troubled electric air of the fishing village where she had had Mina alone to herself for perhaps the last time. She sighed at the memory, then turned away blushing as she remembered their playful games.

In her present dreams, Lucy often found herself trapped, lying naked and helpless under the onslaught of some dark figure while being pierced through and through as if by large hot needles. Now she awoke from such a dream, her body tingling from its exertions to be free. She stretched and as she did so there was a tapping at her door. It opened to let Mrs Fraser (and her beast) slip through just as the sun was sinking from the sky. She sat beside the still-dazed girl and in the gathering darkness made smalltalk. Then with a sigh of 'at last' she tugged off her bonnet to reveal her pale face and hair. She turned her burning gaze on the figure of the girl, much like a carnivorous animal might on its prey. Then her hands were pushing up the shift Lucy had been sleeping in and pulling it over her head. Lady Augustus had sat up for the latter, and now completely naked she flushed a deep startled pink which made the woman even more assertive.

Lucy was a willing, but submissive participant. To emphasise her complete subjection, Mrs Fraser tied the girl's hands and feet to the bedposts with scarves. She glared down at her spread-eagled victim as she stripped off her own bulky garments. Naked, she sat beside Lucy, gently stroking her cheek, before parting the girl's blonde flowing hair to reveal the pulsing vein at the side of her neck. Lucy's helpless eyes stared up at the woman's face as she felt the fingers pressing against the jugular vein through which her blood soared in anticipation. She moaned as the woman's lips and then other lips touched her skin. She had forgotten about the dingo.

The imprisoned girl writhed, but not to be free. At the extent of her vision, at her loins, was the thin tawny animal lapping away with a long tongue that, sweeping in and out of her, made her body squirm. The sensations were of such strength that she did not at first cognise the lips at her throat turning into hard teeth, two of which were as sharp as needles. This she knew suddenly, as they bit down. She felt the blood spurting from her and into a mouth clamped about her wound just as her body spasmed and spasmed. She gave a piercing scream and then went limp, content only to be fed on.

The government mission was of a minor nature which Sir George Augustus, bored in England, had been urging his patron in Bath to get for him. Now he and his new wife had voyaged to this distant and most obscure colony of Westland whose only settlement was a squalid collection of shacks clustered about a few substantial buildings below a rise on which the governor's house squatted: a dak bungalow transported from India with rooms opening onto a surrounding verandah. Although it might have served for a waystation for company officials in India, it lacked the dignity of a seat of government and so the governor, at his wife's urging, had commenced a more substantial dwelling, which after a lengthy correspondence had been sanctioned by London. At the moment only the foundations had been dug, for all work had come to a standstill with the egress of almost the entire male population from the town.

The dwelling indeed was small even for the limited affairs of the colony. The largest room, which had to serve as a dining room, drawing room, library and often as the governor's office, was crowded with bulky furniture. A piano stood in one corner and in the other the governor's desk. A bookcase leaned against another wall, and there was a sofa, two easy chairs and a small table with a large leather armchair beside it, which might have been termed the governor's residence, for in it he sat for hours at a time, sipping on brandy when he could get it, or rum bartered from the ships when he could not. There he sat like a Hindoo yogi contemplating nothing, except when he became the harassed husband; then he thought about how to avoid his wife, Rebecca Crawley, who had never grown used to being exiled at the edge of the known world. She lamented her evil fate much too often for his comfort and when it had grown too overbearing he had petitioned the colonial office for a better posting. These requests were acknowledged, and that was all, for in truth the obscure posting was the result of Rebecca Crawley's own misdeeds and had been engineered to get her as far away from the capital as possible, to put a stop once and for all to her meddling in affairs above her station.

Now, the unhappy woman arranged herself on the sofa in her once sumptuous finery, an evening dress of a heavy velvet material which draped her hips in countless folds while leaving her shoulders bare. With a weary shrug, she tossed her black hair – often dyed, now streaked with grey, but still carefully arranged to dangle curls about her narrow fox-like face – and leaned back attractively as her deep dark eyes studied the man who held the floor. His small dainty feet, shod in Bond Street leather, supported his short sturdy legs, while he pronounced on colonial policy in which the Crawleys had not the slightest interest. To distract herself, Rebecca Crawley stared brazenly at his rather coarse features, which were marred, if that was possible, by eczema scars. She wondered what had become of the world when such men as he reached a prominence of sorts and strutted about the empire as if they personally had created it. They achieved what no ambitious woman could in such a world. Look what had happened to her. Merely for taking an interest in politics, she had been exiled to the periphery of all that was modish and powerful in the world.

'Such is my fate as a woman,' she murmured, and sighed as she continued to stare at the man.

Sir George Augustus was one of those self-made knights who, with the Reform Act of 1832, had risen from the enfranchised lower classes, though he had yet to create a suitably noble genealogy to go with his advancement. Hence his family was completely unknown to Mrs Crawley. She, using brazen invention together with her beauty and sharp intelligence, had glossed over her own origins, which were lower than those of the knight; her husband's family was of ancient lineage which she, supposedly a distant cousin, had rejoined through their union. Now she daintily but saucily yawned without putting a hand over her rosebud mouth while the *parvenu* explained how the government of the day, under some compunction from concerned Christians centred on Exeter House, had formed a committee to inquire into the conditions of the natives within the acquisitions of the empire. It had appointed commissioners to report on their wellbeing. He was one of these and had been sent to this colony as he possessed some knowledge of the natives of the Great South Land, of which the colony was the western end. The governor greeted this information with a stolid expression which revealed not even his complete lack of interest. As an old soldier, he believed that as long as the natives stayed quiet that was a good enough condition for him and for the settlers. Under the pressings of the colonial office, however, he had taken a step to elevate the natives, and to control them, through the formation of a native police detachment.

In regard to the indigenous inhabitants, his wife wished them to be out of sight as well as mind. It was she who had had her husband promulgate a decree which forbade them the environs of the town, after they had hovered about like flies around her carriage and laughed at her appearance. Of course, they were still there, snatching up scraps and demanding food; but with the native police about to begin regular patrols, those who still persisted in lurking about the town, their nakedness now covered by dirty blankets or cast-off clothing, would be driven away to distant camps. This was only good and proper, she thought, for really they had no business about the town. Such a dirty, dirty, lazy lot, existing as they always had existed at the very bottom of the scale of civilisation. Why, they had been worth only a line or two in the letters she used regularly to send home, and now not even a line. Her eyes glazed as she lost her focus on the knight who was engaged in a boring monologue which went on and on. She sighed, wishing that her hearing was impaired. All too soon, he had become part of the tedium she had to endure in this wretched colony. She closed her eyes; but alas not her ears.

Annoyed, she opened her eyes to survey the creature again. He was (and she was an expert at detecting them) a rogue out for his own advancement, and thus of more interest than if he had been merely one of those bores who held to a subject from belief rather than duplicity. She sighed as she regarded him, and it was then that a scream ripped apart his monologue. It brought welcome distraction, though not excitement. It lacked the desperate appeal of a call for speedy relief from serious danger. 'Murder, murder!' would have been more diverting.

'That was quite a din. Not the natives, I hope,' observed Governor Crawley, lifting up his glass and taking a gulp of the excellent brandy his guest had thoughtfully provided. 'They do intersperse their yabber with shrieks.'

'Yes, sometimes they do,' partially agreed Sir George. 'Then, some birds make almost human sounds; I have heard the curlew scream in the wilderness like a woman in agony. But this has erupted from my sweet wife. She is not used to these new lands and doubtless it was a bat or some such nightlife that startled her. Silly little thing, she'll be along directly with a contrite expression on her face. Now, as I was saying, the natives if they are to become a source of labour must first be civilised and Christianised. There can be no other way –'

'That shriek from your wife ...' Mrs Crawley broke in, keen to put an end to the native problem. 'I have heard such commotions before and they are not exclamations of fright, far from it.' And she smiled a leering kind of smile which the knight caught, then evaded.

'Well, be that as it may, Mrs Fraser – who has taken a fancy to her – will calm her down. Such a capable woman. One who has seen and experienced much since suffering shipwreck upon these shores,' the husband commented, before returning to his topic. 'There is a shortage of labour here and there are natives enough to alleviate it. Why, you only have a single serving woman to see to your needs. In other colonies with a native population, Colonel, you have servants aplenty. They need to be put to work.'

'Yes, except the beggars won't work,' observed the governor. 'If they did they *would* be working, for recent events have deprived us of male labourers, including my own who came with us. In fact, the situation has become so desperate that I am in the process of petitioning the colonial office for convicts to be transported here. They will provide labour enough and we won't need to use these savages. Other colonies have derived benefit from transportation –'

'No, no,' Sir George exclaimed. 'I strongly advise against it, Governor. To import criminals is not a solution, but only an addition to your problems. Use the natives. Instil in them good work habits and that is your answer. We have only to take the example of our own poor –'

'Well, it may be an evil, but it is one that we will have to embrace. The savages are lazy and –'

'Colonel, I have been a free settler in a penal settlement and the state of affairs I found there is not a fit subject for delicate ears. Even if a convict is sent out for a trifling offence, under the direction of his fellows he soon becomes an adept in crime. It is with the greatest difficulty that they are brought to justice. They league together and even have a vulgar language of their own and they plunder whatever comes their way. The only way to make them work is through the liberal application of the lash, and this too merely hardens them. They are the scourge of a new colony, Governor! Let me relate a trifling episode to show you what they are like.

'It was a scene which defies description,' Sir George began, lowering his voice from its usual high-pitched whine. 'Church on Sunday, and I to deliver an exhortation, but was there a sign of repentance? Could you expect it from such as they? Those who were in irons came in first, pouring in, pushing, pulling and crowding each other in a horrible cacophony of blasphemy, Colonel; abominable obscenity from those who had descended to the level of beasts and so were chained as beasts. And when I began my exhortation the noise subsided, it is true, but to a low hum of voices which, as I continued, rose on occasion to drown out my words. It was a scene from hell and if you bring such creatures here, this is what you can expect.'

'How terrible for you, Sir George,' commented Rebecca sardonically. 'You must have felt like Daniel being thrown into the den of lions.'

'The whip, sir, the lash; it keeps order,' muttered the governor. 'It serves the army well. I know it, for I have ordered it.'

'Colonel, if you persist in your petition, you must raise a gibbet too,' Sir George stated flatly. 'They are hardened to the lash and at least a rope removes the main culprits; though even in the face of death some of the rogues remain defiant, not only to authority but to their very Maker as well.'

Governor Crawley raised a weary hand to his rough chin. A damn good barber was what he needed. He took a sip from his glass, then said absently: 'It may not do now since gold has been discovered in the east. But the labour problem – there is a need for a decent barber and well-trained servants. Are savages capable of being trained for such duties? We need another Sergeant Barron to get them in condition.'

'Gold!' exclaimed Sir George. 'Did you say gold?'

'Yes, and here is gold indeed along with silver,' the governor muttered, suddenly perking up, as at the door appeared first Lady Lucy then a transformed Mrs Fraser.

The change between the dour day image of the woman and her sparkling night self was startling in its extreme. The sun was long gone and along with it her heavy widow's weeds. She had borrowed one of Lucy's cool muslin creations, beneath which her body moved naturally as she had disdained the girl's efforts to get her into stays, protesting that her rigid upright posture and firm figure did not call for such confinement.

'Nor does yours,' she had told her companion, but the decorous young wife felt that she could not appear without them in public.

'It's fun getting tied in,' she mused, 'and if they are tight enough, you're always breathless.' Lucy got her new friend to lace her up, using the operation for many a caress until Amelia warned that time was passing and they had to make an appearance in the drawing room.

Now she tripped in on soft slippers, holding her companion's arm. They stopped in the centre of the room, the cynosure of all eyes.

'My, you look like sisters,' exclaimed Sir George, pushing away the idea of gold to fasten his eyes on another gold – the locks of his wife in a heavy chignon. Then he switched his gaze to Mrs Fraser whose pale, almost white hair flowed freely to set off the delicacy of her features. He noticed that her face was somewhat flushed, her cheeks appearing like pink roses on a field of pure snow, and could not but think that she was a rare beauty; that is, until he met the coldness of her gaze and revised his opinion. Her eyes were the cold blue of sapphires, but reddened in the whites from some malady, which must be that which forbade her skin the touch of the sun. She was all pale hues and as cool as snowfields under a distant moon.

'If not sisters, at least friends beyond the good, for already I love her,' Lucy declared, dimpling prettily and giving a curtsy to the men, one slender white hand clasped around the alabaster arm of her companion. She appeared pale, though there seemed a radiance beneath the pallor that suggested she might blush at any time. The governor's wife stared enviously from one to the other. Experience narrowed her eyes before she managed to uptilt the corners of her lips in a smile. Such things as she imagined were out of place in this godforsaken colony, though there had been that shriek of ecstasy. Even if that Amelia Fraser seemed about as passionate as an icicle, she had once been captured by savages and held at the mercy of their powerful lusts.

'I thought I heard you scream,' Sir George said to Lucy with a smile, speaking to hide the lapse of manners on the part of the governor as he pulled himself belatedly from his chair to greet the entrance of the women.

'Oh, you know me and my little upsets. It was only Amelia's – Mrs Fraser's – dog. The silly thing sprang at me and put me in a panic. I thought it was about to attack, but it only gave me a good licking. Yuk, and it's so difficult to get warm water here. I feel positively defiled.'

'They got on famously,' Amelia observed. 'It is not often that my dog takes so readily to someone; but have no fear, I have brought him to heel.'

'Oh, he's a good doggy,' Lucy pouted back. 'Such a slobber he made over me.'

'Please, come and sit by me,' Rebecca broke in, jealous at how much attention the two fresh young women were receiving and wanting some of it for herself. 'We do not stand on observance here and your costumes, though suitable to the climate, in other places would be too, too flippish for evening wear.' And she shifted in her seat, calling attention to her own apparel which, if not *de rigueur*, was the correct attire for that time of day.

Lucy giggled when she glanced at the governor's lady. She turned to her companion and made a *moue*. She had not seen a dress so out of fashion, except on older ladies, and this again brought forth the giggle as she tugged on her new friend's arm to take her to the two chairs which were close to Mrs Crawley. The lady indicated the near one for her and she obliged, wishing that the woman had not occupied the couch, for she and Amelia might have sat pressed together indeed like two sisters or – and Lucy raised a slight blush – like she and Mina used to do.

'Now, my dear,' Mrs Crawley said pleasantly and maliciously. 'Relate to me the incidents not of your voyage but of the past season in London. I know that you are not acquainted with the highest society, but it is well reported in the newspapers. Do you know that we were intimates of Lord Steyne? And oh, the balls and receptions I used to attend.' And so she went on and Lucy had to listen, though every now and again she managed to give Amelia's arm a squeeze.

With the ladies settled on their side of the room and engaged in conversation, the impatient Sir George returned to his new topic of interest.

Governor Crawley stroked his chin, listened, stared at his glass, looked up at the ceiling, which was of hessian stretched across the rafters, sighed as he set his thoughts into motion and then his thoughts into words. 'Dashed unlucky for the colony, if you ask me. Dashed unlucky, what with our small population. Just getting on our feet and all that. Didn't think of gold when I sanctioned that expedition by Bailey. Look for good sheep and cattle country, not gold, I told him. That's where the real wealth is, you know. Pastoralism. Get some good estates going. Mutton, beef, straight to India. Wool too. Leather. Excellent prospects, excellent, and trade for some coolies. Indentured labourers, just like slaves, but under contract –'

'Yes, but about this discovery of gold,' broke in Sir George, raising his voice to a squeal which irritated an answer from any listener it was directed at.

'Ah yes, gold, more trouble than it's worth. Bailey was to mount an expedition and make a track eastwards. Set up some depots for others to follow on. Survey and report on the prospects of the country. Did that, he did. Good man. Yes, dry as a bone. Couple of waterholes along the way. Dug them out. Dismal country. Natives, buck naked, pretty wretched too. God knows what they live on. Got him enough drays, carts to carry supplies to set up the depots. Provisions too. Well planned. No problems. Bit of forage about the water, not much though, and no game to speak of. Adventurous cuss, that Bailey. Shook his hand when he set out. Shook his hand when he came back. Grand sight, him going off. Stretching out like an army supply line. Less grand when he returned, though.'

'And the gold, man?' squealed Sir George.

The governor ignored the ill-mannered intervention and continued on. 'Well, it was him that found the dashed stuff. Rather, he came back with a lump of what I thought was copper ore. Just copper. Big hunk of stone. Used it for a door stop, thought nothing of it. When this fellow, forget his name, he came to see me on some business or other. Botheration, but he knew ores and rocks and suchlike things. He's with me, drinking up the last of my brandy, when his eyes go to it. He picks it up, scrapes at it a little with a knife, then declares that it is gold. "Gold?" I ask and he replies, "Gold, and a good essay too." And he wants to know where it was found and, like a confounded fool, I tell him. Too much work involved if it got out. Only realised that after and I got him to promise not to mention it. Word of a gentleman and all that. Well, there's not many gentlemen about when there's gold to be had. He went off after it, and not only that, but the whole town got wind of it and followed. Now the male population is out there. Only women and children left, sir. Only women and children. Even the shopkeepers are there, making more than a pretty penny. Dashed shame, and just when the colony was picking itself up too.'

'Gold, gold,' Sir George said, his voice dropping dramatically and his eyes shining with sudden greed. 'Gold,' he repeated in a whisper before recollecting himself. He puffed up as he assumed his official role. 'Governor Crawley,' he stated. 'I'm afraid that this gives a different perspective to my mission. I had thought that the population of this colony would slowly increase and thus not upset the natives too much; but if gold has been discovered, this means that hordes of riffraff and rascals will descend upon them. Ruffians who will not hesitate to mistreat and take mean advantage of those poor wretches living in their desert fastnesses far from aid and succour. They must be protected, sir, and I am here on behalf of the government to see that they are protected.'

'Hem, report wasn't it? Just a report.'

'It was and still is, Colonel Crawley, and to do that report properly, I must see for myself this ... this goldfield.'

'That's easier said than done, man. The dashed area is somewhat far from here. Hardship, sir, hardship. Too much for a type like yourself.'

'Governor, I have tracked through worse wilderness to get to such wretched creatures as these. To fulfil my mission, I am ready and willing to endure trials and tribulations that might make a lesser man quake. But with your cooperation and goodwill, perhaps an expedition, similar to the one you sanctioned for Bailey, is needed. You have read my commission and it calls for your utmost aid and help. Colonel, an expedition is needed. I know that the committee will defray the costs of such a necessity.'

'But dash it, man, where am I to get the men? All the buggers – excuse me, ladies – all the blighters are at the goldfield already. Those who are left I can't spare.'

'There must be some available who can accompany me. Soldiers, policemen? They could not leave their posts. Desertion is still a hanging matter, is it not?'

'No, old boy, sorry about that. But wait: by deuce, there is a batch of fellows just sitting around. You know, being civilised and all that. A detachment of native police here. Twenty fine fellows. They don't know what gold is and they are well trained by Sergeant Barron, a soldier first and last. I've seen him put them through their paces. Believe me, they can do the job and, best of all, they can be spared. Was going to use them to keep the natives out of town, but what matter if the womenfolk are scared? Maybe that'll bring their menfolk home.'

'And they can drive carts and ride horses, shoot guns and obey orders?'

'They can do these and more under their sergeant. And not only are there these, but Bailey had a native guide – what was his heathen name? Montgomery, or some such. He's given up his heathen ways and carries about a Bible, though he can't read a word of it. He will be your guide. Just say that Jesus has commanded it and he's your fellow. Into the wilderness, eh? Why not.' And the governor almost rubbed his hands in glee to have gotten rid of the visitor so easily.

'So, I can mount my expedition of mercy and compassion as soon as it is feasible – in a few days,' Sir George Augustus replied; and he too might have rubbed his hands together in satisfaction, if he had not glanced at Rebecca Crawley and detected a gleam in her eye.

'I sincerely trust that your mission of mercy will meet with satisfaction, for all of us,' she said, smiling at him as if aware of the hidden purpose beneath his concern. 'I too would accompany you, but alas I fear the dangers and discomforts would be too much for a woman of my constitution and station.'

It was then that Mrs Fraser made a sudden decision, for she also was interested in the gold, and the virile miners. 'I too have the wellbeing of the natives at heart,' she declared. 'Their interests are to a great extent my interests, as they should be for all of us. They, it is true, held me captive in durance vile, but as a Christian I have forgiven them. "Forgive them, Father, for they know not what they do", and are we not ordained by that blessed providence to bring the Word to everyone, even to those who exist in the most degraded of states? I have the strength and determination to accompany you on your noble mission, sir.'

'But, madam,' Sir George protested shrilly, 'you are a woman and such an expedition is not for such as you. In short, it is man's work.'

'No, no,' Lucy said, twisting her face up and clutching Amelia's arm fiercely. 'I could not bear it if you were gone from me. I won't let you go.' And she pressed her face into the shoulder of her friend.

'Piffle,' declared the governor's lady loudly. In truth, she could not bear Mrs Fraser and her hard stare. Having the woman on her hands over the weeks the expedition would be gone was perhaps the most disagreeable thing she could imagine and so she again said 'Piffle' before going on. 'What one sex can do another can also attempt. Was there not Frau Isa Pfeiffer, the world traveller, who enduring great hardships voyaged around the world? I keep her book constantly by my bed as an inspiration of what our sex can do. Sir George,' she commanded, tapping her fan irritably against her wrist, 'Mrs Fraser, who also has had experience among these savages, is well able to attempt this expedition. In fact, it is not into unknown wilderness that you penetrate, for the gold discovery has created such a rush of men into that remote part of our colony that it is remote no longer. Surely, a woman may travel where men have gone!'

'But –' began the knight.

'Sir George,' Mrs Fraser said quietly, gaining his attention and his glance. She held them steadily as she continued: 'I have not told you that I dabble in the pictorial arts and that, in hearing of your adventures, I have attempted a number of sketches which perhaps you shall correct for me one day. I know only the mainland natives, and your experience was in the island to the south. Please examine them, for one of the reasons I wish to accompany you, though the road be hard, is to capture you at work. I feel that that in itself is a noble enterprise, especially if your report, or other publications which might follow, need to be – I would not say embellished – illustrated. I, alas, am all alone in the world and must make my way in as gentlewomanly a fashion as possible.'

So saying, Amelia left her chair, picked up a sketch pad which she had left on the piano and carried it to Sir George. He took it from her gingerly and then clumsily dropped it so that it fell open. He bent over, examined the revealed sketch, then picked the pad up and thumbed through it, stopping every so often as a page caught his fancy. Studying these, now and again he looked up at the woman to say, 'That is not exactly right'. Or, 'Certain details are lacking.' At last, he closed the pad and handed it back to her, commenting as if he were the master and she the pupil: 'You have a way with the charcoal which I admire. On my expeditions of conciliation, in my journals I made rough drawings, but alas lacked the skill to make them live. If you feel that you have the necessary endurance, you may join my mission to render it in graphic detail. What else may I say when this good lady has added her weight to your request?'

'Thank you for your kindness,' Amelia replied somewhat smugly. 'I take it that I am to accompany the expedition as the official artist?'

'Dash it,' exclaimed the governor. 'She is a female and what is more has an aversion to the direct rays of the sun. I do not believe that I can allow this. If something should happen to this lady, it will not go down well in London. Her sojourn among the natives has elicited much interest there, as well as concern.'

'But Colonel Crawley,' replied Sir George 'we are to have an armed escort, and then I have brought with me an Indian bughi, four wheeled rather than two, which has a hood to shade the occupants from the sun's harmful rays. The lady will ride in this, though I must state that she may accompany me only if the landscape is such that the vehicle may proceed without hindrance.'

'There isn't a track suitable for it,' declared the governor, then added as he came under the hard eye of Mrs Fraser: 'But the land is dashedly flat, as flat as a billiard table, and I suppose where carts can go so can that bughi. India is not noted for the smoothness of its roads, is it?'

'No, that is why I chose such a vehicle,' replied the knight. 'Well, if it is to be, it must be. So, let us pass from this subject and enjoy the company of these delightful ladies. Perhaps they will treat us to a song or two. My good wife has a sweet voice. Some have compared it to that of an angel. Please, Lucille, treat us to a song.'

'I can play the piano tolerably well too,' said a petulant Lucy, who since her protest had withdrawn from the subject of the expedition.

Her eyes, swimming with tears, accused her friend of desertion; but proud of her skill she went to the piano, sat in front of it and ran her fingers over the keys. It was somewhat out of tune, but no one called attention to it and she didn't care. She banged out a discordant chord which suited her mood, then looked around and said: 'When we were taking ship, I brought this broadsheet which was to warn young girls about the perils of the South Land. I have not found such dangers here, but then, thank God, I am not one of those poor creatures sent to languish at the ends of the earth.' She flung a glance at her friend, attempted an introduction, then using the out-of-tune piano sparingly began to sing:

'Come all young girls, both far and near, and listen unto me,
While unto you I do unfold what proved my destiny.
My mother died when I was young, it caused me to deplore,
And I did get my way too soon upon my native shore.'

Her clear young voice rose into a lament and everyone listened, though not with the same feelings. Mrs Crawley found the sentiments tedious and her husband soon lost interest. Sir George disliked the subject matter and wished that his young wife had chosen a more fitting song. It was only Amelia who seemed to appreciate the ballad and tapped out the time on her wrist. Then, as the song ran its course, she got to her feet and went to stand beside the singer. The girl, still out of sorts, scowled up at her grumpily before shaping her quivering lips into a little sad smile and thumping out the melody. Both sang out the final verses in a charming duo.

'Come all young men and maidens, do bad company forsake,
If tongue can tell our overthrow it will make your heart to ache;
Young girls I pray be ruled by me, your wicked ways give o'er,
For fear like us you spend your days upon this weary shore.'

'A noble sentiment,' observed Rebecca sardonically. 'It would have done well for me if I too had heeded such advice; but enough of this levity. I remember a similar simple melody which I sang to my sweet child when last I saw him. How I miss him.' She wiped away a fanciful tear before adding: 'It was well received by Lord Steyne. Ah, those joyful, happy days, and so, like the convict lass, I shall sing my mournful lay.'

She rose from the sofa, arranged the voluminous folds of her skirt, then went to the piano, took Lucy's place and sang:

'The rose upon the balcony the morning air perfuming
Was leafless all the wintertime and pining for the spring;
You ask me why her breath is sweet and why her cheek is blooming.
It is because the sun is out and the birds begin to sing.'

Mrs Crawley's voice, it must be admitted, still retained some sweetness; but since the time she had sung the lyric to the appreciation she had described, it had dropped and the song was pitched too high for her. Still, she sang on to the end and curtsied to the polite applause.

'Such beautiful sentiments,' declared Sir George. 'And so well projected that one would think oneself listening to an opera diva.'

'Oh, Sir George,' simpered Rebecca. 'It brings a tear to my eye when I think of my once life. Here, there is nothing but harshness, a dreary harshness in which I languish.'

'May you soon return to those pleasure groves in which you roamed,' Sir George said with some feeling. He turned away as her eye lingered on his, then thinking awhile, he returned to that dark gaze and said: 'I have been so concerned about those poor creatures that I have quite forgotten my wife. She is too delicate to essay the parched hinterland. I must find a place for her and a companion whilst I am on my journey of mercy.'

'Sir George, I am at your service,' quickly replied Rebecca. 'Fear not, your life's companion shall reside safely here whilst you brave the perils of your expedition. Such a soft dove needs a shelter and she shall have it here with me.' And putting action to words, she turned and embraced Lucy, who had not been asked for her opinion or assent.

'And so it is decided,' Sir George said. 'Lucy, you shall find a home here while I am on my travels. And as I have some excellent wine, we shall raise our glasses to the success of my expedition. Lucy, go and get two bottles of the claret.'

His wife obeyed and when she was passing through the door, Amelia slipped out behind her. They had gone along the verandah only a few steps when the girl, with a little cry, flung herself into her friend's arms.

'I don't want you to go,' she cried petulantly. 'I won't let you go.'

'Hush, child,' Amelia replied, stroking her cheek. 'When you are lonely, think of me and I shall be in your dreams.'

'But I don't want to be with that horrid old woman either. She smells of mothballs and dust. I want your smell. It's ... it's ...' and not finishing her sentence she tugged her friend's head down and tried to push her lips against her neck.

'No, child, no,' Amelia whispered, gently detaching herself from the embrace. 'Now get the wine and when you return make excuses for me, say that I am indisposed or at prayer, or some such thing.' And she slipped away, leaving Lucy alone except for a soft wet nose that slipped into her hand.

'And I expect that you are going too,' she exclaimed in mock anger at the dog. 'Well, poof, who cares! I shall be as Clotho, the youngest Fate, and embroider a tapestry with scenes that show your mistress returning to me. I have that piece of canvas and now I shall begin on it when she leaves and continue on until she returns. O let there not be that other Fate, the third, Atropos, who cuts the thread that ends a life. Enough, I mix up the stories. The canvas is there and I will but place thereon the scenes in bright thread. Sweet Mela, I will get her to sketch in the scene for me.'

CHAPTER TWO

Once, the governor and his lady wife had added the *bon* to the *ton;* but that was years ago in the metropolis. In his scarlet jacket and plumed hat, Colonel Crawley, Governor of Westland, still looked resplendent, at least from. a distance. When one came closer, the shabbiness of his furnishments became apparent, though one had to admit that he looked a fine figure, as did his wife. Rebecca was costumed in a fine day dress and a bonnet with a profusion of flowers; but her apparel, even to a casual glance, had seen better days, as had the wearer of them. The *bon* had long deserted the *ton*.

Still, they stood upright and seemingly self-possessed as the detachment of native police in their kepis, dark coats with silver buttons and shining boots trotted behind Sir George's bughi, which (newer and better equipped than the governor himself, not to mention his carriage) approached them. Sir George, clad in a dark frock coat and with his head bare, though beside him rested a wide-brimmed planter's straw hat, held the reins loosely and kept his eyes fixed ahead. Beside him was the heavily draped figure of Mrs Fraser. As her face was completely veiled, it was impossible to see the direction of her gaze; but a slim spectator, clad in the whitest of flimsy white, had no doubt that Amelia's eyes were on her. Lucy fluttered a hand in loss, and drooped like a daisy under a warm breeze as the vehicle passed. Now she let her glance linger on the native police troop, headed by a solitary white man whose stout figure bounced in a somewhat ungainly fashion on his mount, though the fierce florid face with its sweeping salt-and-pepper moustache was enough to quell any criticism. He was an old soldier from the ranks who had fought at Waterloo in the infantry, and had come to his position only after a lifetime of active service.

Sergeant Barron was as proud of his native recruits as he had been of his regiment. As he came abreast of the governor he shouted out: 'Eyes right!' The black policemen obeyed the command in perfect unison. The governor grunted in appreciation and then waited for the eight heavily laden drays to roll past. Each was driven by a police trooper who had tethered his horse behind. The line was long, but eventually it cleared the town and headed for a gap in the escarpment which led up to the flat inland plateau.

The expedition was to have had an early start, but punctuality was not part of colonial life. In fact, once, some time ago, the clocks had all run down and they had been without time until the next ship arrived. Time was flexible and, what with one thing or another, it was noon by the time the expedition had assembled. Then there was a wait for the governor to arrive, and after that they had passed in review and trundled from the town along a rough rutted track which was considered a high road. This meandered through the coastal plain and then up a rise leading to the pass onto the flat inland plateau. At the head of the pass, Sir George stood up in the bughi and held up his hand to halt the line of vehicles behind him. He cast his eyes about, examining the country and finding not much to observe. The land was flat and featureless, the melancholy rutted track disappearing into the eastern horizon.

He motioned the column forward then sat with a thump and shook the reins. They proceeded along the track and continued on until, as the sun was sinking, he decided it was the appropriate time to camp. He summoned the commander of the police to him and gave the necessary order. It was then that Sergeant Barron came into his element, shouting at some of his men to unharness and unsaddle the horses, then hobble them before turning them loose to forage for what grass there was. The remainder he ordered to set up camp, pitching the tents in a single row, at the head of which was his own and a short distance away those of the two civilians. By that time the mess had been set up and the native cook had his fire blazing while he prepared the food.

Sergeant Barron, when he had everything as he liked it, well ordered and spick and span, strode to where Sir George was sitting in his canvas folding chair, removed his kepi and lowered his voice to a rough growl as he said: 'Would have liked to have got a bit further along, but the late start kiboshed it. Tomorrow, up at the crack of dawn and on the road by sun up. With that, we'll make the waterhole; at least, so Monaitch assures me and what he says agrees with Bailey's chart.'

'Ah, yes, the Bailey expedition guide,' Sir George replied. 'I must have a word with him. I have heard that he is a convert.'

'He is and it's to the good and to the bad. Ready to obey a command, but his Jesus that and his Jesus this gets a mite overbearing, if you get my meaning.'

Sergeant Barron was about to add more to this effect, when he stopped, for his listener's face had turned purple. Sir George's voice shrilled as he retorted: 'No, Sergeant, the meaning I get is good news indeed. In my time I have been a lay preacher, and the Word of God is not to be despised, nor are those who open themselves to our Lord and

Master, Jesus, the very Son of God who came down to save each and all of us.'

'Well, I'll add my amen to all that, sir. I'll send him along directly after we have eaten. Perhaps you can share a hymn or two,' Barron replied, with a carefully neutral expression to which the knight could not take exception. The police sergeant turned to go, then looked over his shoulder and said: 'Take it you're prepared to eat police grub. Got one of my boys trained in what you might call the culinary arts. His food is basic, but filling. I'll send over a plate for you and the lady.'

Sir George nodded, falling into the romantic past of his previous journeys, and when the plate of salt pork and beans was placed before him he ate with a gusto he had not felt for some time. He had invited Mrs Fraser to share his humble repast but did not notice that she merely pushed her food about on the plate, then fed it to her canine companion before excusing herself and going into her tent. She emerged with her drawing pad and quickly sketched the camp scene. There in the foreground sat Sir George in his canvas collapsible chair.

'Ah, the first record,' he said, eyeing the sketch, and then suggested that she might do another in a little while when he was communicating with the native constables. He wanted it when the sun was setting and long shadows streaking across the campsite. 'Put in a tree or two, for I see that there is none that will give me the effect I desire.' She nodded to this and, when the time came, followed him to Sergeant Barron who shouted as they approached: 'Monaitch, on the double!'

A native clad in ragged shirt and canvas trousers ran towards them.

'Civilian black, sir. Not one of mine at all and not eligible for a police issue of clothing,' the police sergeant explained. Then, angry at such raggedness and shabbiness, he growled: 'If the blighter put in a day or two's work, what with everyone off to the diggings, he might dress like a king. Get them to ride or shoot all right, but an honest day's labour, not on your nelly.'

'All right, Sergeant, that will be enough.' Sir George scowled as he added: 'And he is working now, as my guide, and what's more he is a Christian and when the occasion arises, I myself shall clothe him.'

'Very good,' Barron replied, his face carefully blank.

Monaitch stood before Sir George clutching a Bible. Proudly, he held it out towards the knight. 'I carry Word of God,' he intoned. 'I cannot read, for he who was about to teach me was murdered by those who refused to accept Jesus as their Lord and Saviour. Fools, for they are perdition bound. Please, read me chapter and verse, for I hear you are Christian man. Good Christian man, yes? How uplifting, yes, a holy journey, undertaken in furtherance of His work.'

'Yes, yes,' answered Sir George, who once had been called Father by the remnants of a savage people he had instructed in the arts of civilisation and the true religion. He sought to summon up his reserves of piety, but those quaint years of being a father to savages who had ill repaid his efforts were long gone and he had other concerns to pursue now, even though he was ostensibly on a mission of mercy. The old image he now tried to invoke was for Mrs Fraser and her ready sketch pad.

'I will preach to all of them,' he declared, turning to her. 'It will be a good picture, the light dawning in their dusky faces as I exhort them to forgo their cruel savagery.'

'They've already done that. Good boys now, the lot of them,' Sergeant Barron commented, defending his men.

'But do they accept Jesus Christ as their Lord and Saviour?' Sir George replied testily, staring at the soldier who, for all he knew, could be as much in need of saving as any of the blackfellows under him.

'That I wouldn't know, but they accept me as their chief and the police as their new tribe,' rejoined the sergeant. 'That is what the governor wanted me to do and I did it. They're loyal now and true to their uniform and me –'

'Jesus alone is my Lord and Saviour,' Monaitch intoned, breaking in to end the policeman's words. He knelt and rattled off in a sing-song voice: 'Therefore, accursed Devil, acknowledge your condemnation, and pay homage to the living and true God; pay homage to Jesus Christ, His son, and to the Holy Spirit, and depart from these servants of God, for Jesus Christ, our God and Lord, has called them to His holy grace. Accursed Devil, never dare to desecrate the holy sign of the cross. Through the same Christ our Lord, who is to come to judge the living and the dead and the world by fire.'

'Amen, amen,' called Sir George, shrilly. For some reason, he felt himself disliking the sentiment expressed, and this caused him to wonder from which sect the missionary had come. Still, he felt pleasure in having a convert of such fervour kneeling at his feet and clasping in both hands the cross he wore on a string about his neck. He looked around to see if Mrs Fraser was sketching this touching scene and was disappointed to find that she had disappeared. Well, she could copy it from memory.

Now, with his hand uplifted, he said, 'Rise, my son,' and then began to sing:

'Speed Thy servants, Saviour, speed them!
Thou art Lord of winds and waves:

They were bound, but Thou shall free them;
Now they go to free the slaves.
Be Thou with them:
'Tis Thine arm alone that saves.
Friends, and home, and all forsaking,
Lord, we go at Thy command;
As our state Thy promise taking
While we traverse sea and land:
O be with us!
Lead us safely by the hand.'

'Amen, amen, amen, amen!' shouted the ecstatic Monaitch; but Sir George suddenly felt despondency sweeping over him. Once, he too had radiated such fervour, though into an unresponsive world that over the years had lessened his urges for such enthusiasms. How he longed for that more youthful time and faith, which had powered him through trackless wildernesses seeking out such as those who stood before him. 'Hallelujah, hallelujah,' he had shouted in exultation and those, his children, had shouted back: 'Jesu, Jesu.' Then, then, on fire, but now his heart held only ashes and his mind only greed for the pure gold. Gold, yes, gold, the soft glowing metal cheered him as well as fevered him. He breathed in deeply and felt that the dust particles in the air were gold, filling him with their power. Now he was ready. He took up the Bible, let it open at a page and read:

'"At that time, as the eleven disciples were at table, Jesus was revealed to them. He reproached them for their disbelief and stubbornness, since they had put no faith in those who had seen him after he had been raised. And he told them, 'Go into the whole world and proclaim the good news to the whole of creation. The man who believes in it and accepts baptism will be saved; the man who refuses to belief in it will be condemned. And signs like these will accompany those who have professed their faith: they will use my name to expel demons; they will speak entirely new languages; they will be able to handle serpents; they will even be able to drink deadly poison without harm; and the sick upon whom they lay their hands will recover.'"

'O Lord, you glow before me like molten gold!' he suddenly shouted, glaring at his flock who, perhaps luckily, were not his flock. They stared back at him ·in puzzlement and he wished to move them as his bright vision had him. His mind returned to the old days and the words of a simple sermon came to him. He began to speak as if in tongues. It was broken English and he pushed his voice up to a shrill to reach into the hearts of each and every one who was listening. 'One good God; one bad Devil. God good to us. He lives in sky and looks down. Devil is bad and lives underground in the fire. Good people who love God will go to Him when they die. All those go along same road, white man and blackfellow. True, true!'

Sir George stopped, for the troopers were staring back at him with blank faces which did not reveal even limited interest in his words. Their leader had a different expression on his face, though he spoke kindly enough: 'Sir, these heathen need someone to instruct them carefully. They know only my commands and what I teach them. Later, they will learn more when missionaries are sent among them. Your words only confuse them. It'll take a while yet, before they are ready for such sermons.'

'Hallelujah,' the irrepressible Monaitch shouted. 'Good, Father, good. Hallelujah!'

'If there is only one prepared to listen, then that is enough; for it is not the size of the congregation that matters, but the faith in their hearts.' And with this Sir George took the arm of the convert. He guided Monaitch to his tent where he talked to him not of God and Jesus, but of the stone streaked with yellow marks which the Bailey expedition had found. 'I need to know about this magic stone if I am to further God's work,' he said, appealing to both the Christian and the savage in Monaitch.

The native screwed up his face. Sir George watched him ponder, then smile. Monaitch laughed in glee as he replied: 'That stone, not magic, but pretty. I found it, liked it and flung it into a dray. No one cared for it, not even that governor. Later, they want to know where it come from. True, true, silly stone. Well, my words not so many then and I mistook their question. I said "Yillarn", which means in our language "rock", and there is a place of that name too where Bailey been. But it not come from there. It come from Kalipa, a place in desert where they live without Jesus.'

'Are there many such stones there, Monaitch?' Sir George asked, placing his hand on the man's shoulder. In his experience, such physical contact was welcomed by blackfellows.

'Many, many, enough to build a big house for God.'

'And I will too, that is a promise to you,' declared Sir George. 'So you know this place?'

'I know this place. Jesus show me the way. He talk to me, He talk to me. He does, He does,' the native shouted.

'He does, I assure you He does,' the knight replied, rubbing his hands together. 'And you can lead us there?'

'Too right I can. Hallelujah, Father, Hallelujah, for the tribe there know not the Lord. He not their Saviour. They believe in giant serpent. Kill it, kill it, for Jesus' sake.'

'The Devil, yes, that is the Devil and he must be unthroned. Monaitch, the Lord has smiled down on you this day.'

When the native guide lifted up his cross, Amelia Fraser, who was preparing to sketch the scene, slipped quickly away from the detested symbol which shone a lurid painful light that blistered her skin. Sir George's words about driving out demons might have made her smile at other times, but the symbol of another's pain had hurt her enough to make her rage that there were such things of torment. The sun dipped below the horizon as she rushed into her tent. At last! She flung off her heavy and constricting clothing, which again reminded her of her mortality, then she transformed into a bat and flapped up into the sky. Her anger left her and she exulted in her mastery of the elements, though she had to keep close to the ground until the sun was well and truly gone and night was a warm refuge about her. Now she rose higher and higher until the land spread out below her as wide and as enduring and as lonesome as her life felt; but she had a friend. She flew a large circle and to the east saw a single dot of red which might be a campfire; but as she completed the arc to the southwest the small collection of lights which marked the town drew her. She darted off towards it.

Except for the drawing room and Lucy's bedchamber, the governor's bungalow was in darkness with nary a figure in sight. Still, Amelia carefully circled the structure before coming down to the lighted window of the girl's room. She fluttered there, beating her wings and hoping to attract her attention. She stopped this when she saw that her friend was not alone. She was conversing with Rebecca Crawley, or rather listening to her. Amelia hung at the window and waited.

The bedchamber, as all the rooms, was overcrowded with furniture. A four-poster bed was pressed against one wall, a dressing table filled a gap between the head of the bed, and a huge mahogany dresser hulked along the wall, covering the bottom half of the window. Against the other wall, leaving scarcely room for the door to open, was a large wardrobe in which Lucy had stacked her husband's and her own clothing in an attempt to keep them from the dust which covered everything. Alongside the bed an Axminster carpet had been laid out. On it were three stuffed easy chairs and pieces of luggage which made the space into an irregular maze.

Lucy sat on the bed, which was perhaps the only comfortable and free place in the room, for the chairs were piled with odds and ends. It also provided enough space for the wooden frame of her embroidery tapestry which was before her though the canvas was still blank. The governor's lady shared her bed, reclining on it and taking up much more space than the girl, who was forced to huddle against the bedhead.

Rebecca Crawley with only Lucy as a guest had stopped any pretence of dressing appropriately for morning, noon and evening. She wore a pink domino, more than a trifle faded and soiled, and marked here and there with pomatum; but her arms shone out from the loose sleeves of the garment, which was tied tightly around her waist so as to set off her still trim figure. As she reclined on one elbow, she sipped on a glass of brandy, thus breaking up into paragraphs the monologue bemoaning her fate.

'Is not this a strange and dismal place for a woman who has lived in a vastly superior world? Was it my fault that I put the interests of my country first and, I admit it, was naive enough to be led on by my Lord Steyne? Politics, my dear, is not for us women, and so alas and to my detriment what was to have been discreet became indiscreet and the subject of vain journalists who slung low jibes in my direction. Calumnies, but they hurt, my dear, they hurt as if I was being struck by arrows and I was too, arrows of outrageous fortune. I, who but followed the dictates of my husband, had to continue to do so when he was shunted off to this post.'

She took a sip of brandy and passed one of Lucy's lace handkerchiefs across her eyes.

'But, alas, it is the lot of women to be alongside their men and I am the truest wife that ever lived. When he was made governor here, I accompanied him, though my heart bled to leave my child, my one darling boy behind; but it was for his own benefit. If he had come with me, he might have become as low as any of these savages. Still, I am as true a mother as I am a wife, and my heart bleeds for him.'

She affected to break down and her sobs filled the handkerchief, though behind the concealing cloth her eyes remained dry.

'O you poor thing,' Lucy declared, 'to be far from hearth and home and the sight of your dear child. I pity you. I couldn't bear it. I have not your strength and devotion.'

'And do not forget the luxuriant salons I frequented. I was in the highest of high, society, kings and princes and ambassadors were at my feet. Alas, to be denied all that; but, my dear, I admit it – I have always been restless and if I am here today, then tomorrow I shall be back among those who are my equals. It will be soon too,' she declared with a tinkle of silvery laughter.

She had another swallow and changed the subject as her mood shifted. 'And you are going to fill in your days with embroidery. Ah, the delicate work I once did and displayed to great appreciation. Pretty pictures of my ancestral home, but I shall not bore you this night with that. I must go to my dear husband.' And taking her now empty glass she wound from bed to door and disappeared with a 'Sweet dreams await you'.

Lucy looked after her and shrugged, turning her attention to her blank canvas. She had failed to get her friend to sketch in a topic and she had not the skill. She knew it; she knew it, and what would she now do to fill in her days? She sighed and fiddled with her wool, then gave a start as from the half-blocked-up window, there came a flapping sound somewhat like a gentle rapping. She tried to lean over the sideboard to peer through. Only the darkness of the night. She sighed again and then suddenly there came again that rapping, but this time it was a gentle tapping at her chamber door. She made a *moue*. Not that old Rebecca Crawley again with her endless sad stories of a once bright life turned as dismal as the colony to which she had been exiled. She could relate to the poor woman, but it did become tiresome to listen on and on. Maybe she should help herself to her husband's brandy and dull the next monologue with it. Again that soft rapping. She meandered her way through the chairs and luggage to the door and opened it to her delight.

'Amelia,' she gasped as the naked woman slipped into her room and into her arms. 'You knew that I was feeling peevish and so came to me. Let me hug you some more. I was languishing, thinking you were far out on that – that trail, as that American I once met persisted in saying, although we had regular roads and streets where we lived.'

'Enough, sweet child. I missed you and could not leave you moping here or me moping there. How dusty and tawdry this place is ... as dusty and as melancholic as the land. Perhaps I have been here too long?'

'What, you just arrived! I won't let you leave after only a hug. If this is all that you have for me, you should have brought your dog. I shiver when I imagine his tongue on and in me, and I a young wife too.'

'Silly, sweet, I meant this land; this end of the earth place. I'll be with you for a little while.'

'Well, it is the ends of the world.'

'It is; but we have each other,' smiled Amelia, manoeuvring Lucy towards the bed.

'Wait, Mela – can I call you that? Once I had a good friend, a chum called Mina, and she was somewhat like you, though not as much fun.

Wait until I am free of my clothing. Help me! I don't want to spot it and I doubt that that woman will be back this night, for she seemed somewhat tipsy. She has a thirst for the brandy.'

'And your Mela has a thirst for you,' replied the woman, unlacing her, then thrusting her down upon the bed and pressing her lips hard against her neck. She kissed the pulsating vein, then thrust her fangs into it. The iron taste of fresh young blood overwhelmed her senses for a long moment, but only until she felt Lucy's throat tighten to emit a shriek. Quickly, she put her hand over the girl's mouth and nose, cutting off her air supply. Lucy's body began bucking as she fought to get air; but Mela, with the hunger on her, continued to deny her blessed relief while she drank up her blood. With the girl slipping away from consciousness, she finally released her.

Lucy lay there shuddering all over. It was as if she had passed through a little death and found that she still endured. At last, her breathing and body settled. Languidly, she turned and pressed herself against her friend's naked body. It was so cool and drew away her own warmth. Timidly, her hand went down past Mela's belly and her fingers brushed her pubic hair. 'You are dry and arid there,' Lucy murmured, 'and I have not the strength to arouse you. Mina used to like my hand doing this to her, but she was so moist.'

'Well, the land out there is dry and arid, and I have only supped on you a little this night. Next time, you shall find me as drenched as you may wish. Now I should be off, for I must get back before the dawn. It was only your sweet self that called me here, and that red foam I find so delicious.'

'But, but you will be back soon, Mela? I swear that I need you more than anything.'

'As soon as it is possible, for the taking of your vital fluid will weaken you. Just build yourself up for my next visit and don't fret. Occupy your days with that embroidery.'

'Well, what am I to do if you are not here? Rub myself raw?' pouted the girl. 'Go away, leave me to mournful solitude. I have decided to be Clotho, the youngest Fate, and embroider a tapestry with scenes that depict your adventures while I suffer alone here. Go away. There is my canvas and there is my wool; they shall be my friends. But wait, I have no picture.'

'Silly, silly goose, you mix up the stories ... and as for that blank canvas. Give it here.'

'See, it is as blank as your heart; and if I mix up the stories, it is because you mix me up. O let me be that other Fate, the third, Atropos who cuts the thread that ends a life. I need you too much to live on alone.'

'Be like Penelope and embroider while you wait.'

'O enough of these silly stories. You will go and I shall cry and then I shall embroider. Leave me something that I may begin. When my needles pierce it through and through, I will imagine your teeth at my neck.'

'Give me the canvas, the night is seeping away. There! This is how the journey began. That is the governor and his wife. Saint George sits in his bughi and a native constable on that dray. It is enough, for that corner. The rest I will sketch in as we go along and I visit you.'

'But where are you? I want you more than them. Your pale hair, your glowing fair face, your azure eyes tinged with the red of the sunset. I want you as you are now, naked and unashamed and flushed with my blood.'

'Let it be, my sweet one; let it be! See in that tree? What is that which hangs there with strange reddened eyes that peer out at the scene?'

'It is a bat. I want you there, Mela!'

'But let that be me, and I'll figure too in the other pictures I shall draw for you. Now I must hasten; but before I go I'll do another scene. There is Saint George, it is but a joke of mine. There is your husband playing the preacher in front of his flock; but where he should clasp a Bible he holds a golden nugget. There, that is your next tapestry scene done. You shall have more as we go along, and when you think of me, look to the picture in which I shall be hidden.'

'Is that you in the darkened sky, obscuring a star?'

'It is, and that is where I soon shall be. Hug me now and I'll lick away the blood which still drips from your lacerated neck ... Now farewell. Ah, you taste so very sweet, like a peppermint. I could easily suck you all away; but, no, there are others. Sweet dreams and in them I shall come to you all moist.'

CHAPTER THREE

A giant man with a huge bushy beard plodded in great heavy boots along the track. His head was down and his shoulders stooped as he maintained a steady pace that moved him ever on towards his goal. He had been so long on the track that he was covered all over with dust, so much so that it was impossible to determine the colour of his clothing or hair. Like a bullock, he was yoked to a load. A leather harness was about his neck and from it straps descended on each side to where his big gnarled hands clasped the wooden shafts of a makeshift wheelbarrow whose body had been made from slabs of timber which slanted away from a big wooden wheel clamped together with iron. This, as it revolved, gave out a long squealing protest. The contraption was piled high with supplies and between the shafts hung two canvas waterbags which, from their flattened appearance, were near empty.

As the head of the expedition approached this figure, Sir George stared at the fellow and declared with some satisfaction: 'Where there is gold, there are such creatures, and they are often easily divested of their gleanings.' He spoke thus to his silent cloaked companion who did not reply. Not being a taciturn man this irked Sir George, and so he directed his voice at the traveller.

'Hey, you, fellow,' he called in his shrill tone which carried a goodly distance. He whipped up his horse to come up closely behind the giant. 'Get off the track, we are on government business.'

The man gave one red-eyed glare over his shoulder, neither breaking his gait nor swerving aside. The knight scowled and would have remonstrated, as he often did with those he considered beneath him, but decided against it. In such flat country, keeping to tracks was a matter of habit rather than of necessity. He pulled the reins to the right and rolled up alongside the man.

'Well, my good fellow,' he declared with the heartiness he assumed when speaking to such ruffians. 'How long do you think you can continue your trek until heat, exhaustion and lack of water claim you?'

'Longer than you, Toffee Nose,' the giant heaved out in a voice raspy and rough from the miles of dust he had stirred up as he trudged along. 'Russian Jack, he don't end up dead before he sights that precious metal. There's water ahead and then there's my mate who could not take to the road shank's pony and picked up a cart for hisself. He's at Yillarn waiting for me. Stupid blighter, couldn't handle his liquor, got into a scrap and went off without me and these provisions. Well, he'll be in for a bit of this.' And he clenched his right fist a few inches above the shaft before grabbing it again. 'Silly bugger, but give him one and settle the score as mates do, then go out and strike it rich. Lodestone for sure, and Russian Jack will be bloody Millionaire Jack.'

'Well, good luck to you and all who traverse this parched land and, as a good Christian, if I find your body on my return, I shall give it a decent burial,' Sir George called down, jocularly.

'And I'll spit on your corpse,' the giant exclaimed, then lowered his face to the barrow and plodded on.

Sir George trundled past him as did the rest of the expedition. They made a wary arc about the giant traveller.

'Amazing, how these fellows get the news,' he said to Mrs Fraser, glancing at the dark figure beside him and hoping for a conversation to emerge which would lessen the fatigue of the journey. 'The secret's just out and already there are rascals like him on the road. The governor will have his work cut out to police such as he, though Crawley's lady wife strikes me as being able to manage anyone, or thing for that matter.'

'Such a giant of a man,' observed Amelia and lapsed back into silence, a hand languidly stroking the neck of her dingo which lay beneath her feet.

In the late afternoon, the expedition reached a spot where the higher level of the ancient plateau still held as two eroded mesas between which the track passed. There was a slight incline, then a descent towards where a soak with some greenish water surrounded by a belt of mud lay in a hollow. Sir George might have let his horse have its head and go into the mud except the presence of a laden wagon bogged there made him pull back on the reins. He would let the water be brought to his thirsty beast.

Sergeant Barron urged his tired horse up to examine the wagon from the edge of the mud, then turned and signalled his troopers. They came up and he pointed at the place where he wanted the camp set up. 'Lone-tree camp according to Bailey,' he stated, 'and the first of his waterholes. Civilians to the left of the tree and troopers to the right. A detail to unload the canvas buckets and water the horses. Get to it!'

Monaitch, who had become Sir George's factotum, saw to his animal. After relieving its thirst, he unharnessed the horse, hobbled it and led it toward a patch of thin grass where it bent its head to snuffle about for a few dried blades. Two black constables unloaded what was needed from the drays; while this was going on, Sir George was occupied with selecting the needful for the night from his own special supplies of goodies, which he had strapped to the back of the bughi.

He watched as Sergeant Barron, lifting his feet high, approached the wagon. The teamster, not being able to extricate it, had lain down in the mud in the shade of the vehicle without bothering to unharness his horses, though footprints in the mud showed that he had watered them before putting on their nosebags.

'You'd better get those animals out of the shafts and out of the mud before they become stuck for ever,' Barron shouted at the man, who got to his feet, went to the wagon and upended his waterbag over his sun-reddened and flaking face without a glance or a reply. After this, he stared at his beasts while he fumbled in his pocket, pulled out a plug of tobacco and a hasp knife, cut off a piece and thrust it into his mouth. He chomped away, calmly regarding the sergeant, who glared at him, his moustache bristling as he shouted: 'Man, you are in the mud and you need us to get you out, so none of your dumb insolence. What's your cartage? And you'd better have permits for what you've got there too. The governor's tightening up, seeing everything's going to the diggings, leaving the town in short supply.'

'Goods for Paddy. Ye know him all right. He's got the inn in town, but now he's opened a grog shop on the diggings. Jesus, those blighters can drink and it's up and down this track all the time for the likes of me. If ye want to see a permit, see him. I'm only the driver, mate.'

'Sergeant to you, and I just hope that his grog shop is licensed. Paddy, from Cork, eh? I've sunk a few jars with him. Barron's the name, late of Her Majesty's army and now of Her Majesty's police, and those blackfellows are my men and just as good as the likes of you. And to whom may I be talking? Should I know you?'

'Naw, I've lately arrived and from one bog to the other, so as to speak. I'll be obliged to ye if ye can get some of yer blacks to tug me out. The nags smelt water. Was dozing and before I knew it, they were away and bog's yer uncle. Hang on a minute, will ye, and I'll unharness the beggars.'

'You just do that and then I'll just glance over what old Paddy has there. Mates, you know; but then I'm a policeman and that takes precedence.'

'His business and his stuff,' the teamster growled, as he unharnessed the four horses and, with a stream of oaths, forced them through the mud to solid ground. 'Now, there's yer mate's wagon. It's heavy and I'm but the driver, not a bloody navvy, though I've had a go at that too.'

'Well, maybe you'll have to do a bit of navvying, if it's to be shifted,' Barron retorted. He shouted for a dozen of his blacks to come to him on the double and ordered them to take off their uniforms and boots. 'Don't want them to get all muddy,' he declared to the teamster.

After a great deal of shoving, the wagon was pushed onto firm ground. Barron ordered his men to wash the mud off and dress. He walked about the vehicle, then lifted the tarpaulin and eyed the contents. 'You think that he would be carting water instead of rum and that rotgut whisky of his. Ah, that's a neat little cask, probably his own private stock and I have the need of such for my water. Tsk, tsk, full it is; but after a time it'll be empty and fit for my purposes. It'll do to wet my gullet until it runs dry. Paddy, he must've known I was on the trek and put it in for me. Naw, not him, but his lady wife, who all on her lonesome welcomes me at the inn. Such a kindly woman, a bit on the big side, but so is her heart. Now I'll just take her a present, eh?'

'Nothing to do with me, but what'll I tell him? Tight as a rooster's hole, he is, and his missus has marked 'em all down. Both of 'em without a word of lettering, but when it comes to their stuff, they know what they got. See this paper here. Those little drawings and strokes are what's on this cart. Anything missing and it'll come out of me five shillings a day. Well, he'll have to abide it this time. Can't do a thing when the constabulary has a hand on his things. Worse come to the worse, I'll tell him to shove it, for I've got me a hankering to try me luck on the diggings.'

'Not a worry, I'll give you a chit to let him know you're on the square. Done him a favour or two. We'll be at the diggings about the same time and I'll tell him myself. Sly grogging is against the law, and he has to pay for it. When a police outpost is established, I'll be in charge and with me sweetened up that'll be worth a drink or two, and there'll be cartage on a government contract, top rates. What's it like out here, anyways? Been too occupied with drilling my boys to get far from the town.'

'Yillarn? Well, there's gold enough, for those who want to dig for it. The surface stuff's gone by now, but I hear tell there's a strike further to the east at a place called Kulgardee Flats. Water's a problem. Needs to be carted in. Sells for two bob a bag, but then this sells for five shillings a mug and does more than wet your throat.'

Barron nodded. He lifted his cask and took it back to where his tent had been set up. The man was still keeping up his blather, but Barron had more than words on his mind. His lips smacked as he entered his tent. Now, away from the eyes of that civilian who had been watching them, he broached the cask and had a long satisfying drink of rum. So satisfying in fact, that he had another before stomping off to oversee the preparation of dinner.

A man's work went smoothly when his joints were oiled and soon

Barron had everyone functioning as he wanted them to; that is, in as disciplined a manner as possible. Now, without a thing to do, he glanced across at the civilian tents where the strange draped lady stood with her dog or whatever, her dingo, sitting beside her. He saw that she was impatient, or out of sorts – though who could blame her, having to wear such clothes in the heat – for there was a slight motion of the bottom of her skirt which showed that she was tapping her right foot. Well, he felt the same way. Out here, from what he could see about him, there was nothing except flat boredom; but then he had his rum. He was about to go again to his nice little cask, when suddenly there was a shout.

The teamster: 'Blacks, blacks!'

Instantly, Barron yelled out for his boys to load. A few spears whizzed at them. 'Fire, one round each!' he shouted.

This put an end to the spears. 'Saddle up,' Barron commanded. 'We'll get on after them. There's that blighter on the road and they might get him. Come on, you lot, chop-chop, hurry up, you know the drill.'

In a matter of minutes, Sergeant Barron had galloped off with a dozen of his troopers and quiet returned to the camp. Sir George and Amelia went to the cursing teamster, who was stumbling about half blinded by blood.

'He's hurt,' Mrs Fraser exclaimed, taking the man's head in her gloved hands. Her face came down to examine the wound through the thick veil, then drew reluctantly away. It had been only a glancing blow, though it had left a nasty gash which bled copiously.

'Fellow, there is a lady present,' the knight snapped.

The teamster left off his swearing and wiped the blood from the side of his head with a dirty rag he had pulled from a pocket. He grimaced at it, then replied: 'Ye know, such is the luck of the Irish. Thought I was safe enough with you lot here, but it's the water. Not much of it about and it draws 'em. Keep on guard if ye camp at water. Forget it and, well, see those spears ...'

'Well, Barron's after them,' Sir George observed.

'Ah, the sun is just about to set,' Amelia said. 'Natives do not attack in the night and so it will be safe for me to do my ablutions. And the darkness will keep me hidden from any eyes as I bathe.' She pushed her veil up over her bonnet, though the deep brim kept her face in shadow, then walked off towards her tent. Her dog got up and followed.

'A cool one for a lady, sir,' the teamster commented. 'Sometimes they get into the hysterics and make more bloody noise than a charge of yelling savages.'

Sir George left him talking and ambled over to the spears. He brought them back to where the teamster was making a fire and examined their construction. They were, he saw, different from those he had known on the south island. Those had been heavier and more like sharpened sticks where these had heads of hard quartz, shaped like a rose leaf and chipped about the edges. The heads were quite well made, but brittle, wedged into a slot at the end of the thin wooden shaft and secured firmly with a binding of string which appeared to be human hair. The head of the one which had struck the teamster had splintered into pieces. Sir George glanced at the fellow, who had wrapped the dirty rag about his head.

The man took Sir George's gaze as a sign to begin blathering again. 'Just a scratch, and the blood would've washed away any poison they used. Thank God I was not stuck like a blasted pig. Had a mate who was speared in the thigh. Ye see that point? When it hits, it splinters. Well, he was struck to the bone and the flint shattered in his flesh. The pieces had to be probed for. Ye should've heard him shouting and screaming, even though he had a whole bottle of rum in him; which reminds me ...' He fumbled under the seat of his wagon and pulled out a bottle which he uncorked. 'Care for a slug?' he said, holding it out.

Sir George took the bottle, wiped the mouth and took a swallow of the fiery liquid. He passed it back and replied: 'These natives, are they mistreated? For in my experience they do not attack without provocation.'

'It's the water, mate, the water –' began the teamster but found that the man's shrill voice was more than a match for his own.

Now he had to listen to Sir George discussing his mission and how the condition of the poor uncivilised blacks could be alleviated. The bottle was finished by the time Sir George had talked himself out. The teamster, with a muttered curse which Sir George took as an apology, stumbled to his wagon and bedded down under it. His snores rumbled out and did not even stop when from the darkness came an eerie creaking noise.

But Sir George was alert. He stared off along the track from where the sound was coming. It grew into a screech, and he was just about to call Monaitch to query him on what strange animal could be making the racket, when a dark mass resolved into the giant figure of Russian Jack, who, without a word, collapsed in exhaustion before him. After a few minutes under the stare of the knight, he recovered enough to kneel and unbuckle his harness.

'No one touch that,' he growled, with a shake of his matted hair and beard at the wheelbarrow. He sniffed the air and his bleary eyes fell on Amelia's plate of untouched food. He crawled over and tipped it over his great gob, gulped, then licked up what remained. Revived by it, he took up his waterbags and plodded off to the soak. There was the sound of splashing, and he returned to his wheelbarrow just as Barron and his native boys walked their tired horses into camp.

'No luck,' shouted the sergeant. 'Look to your mounts, boys, and then see to yourselves.'

This they did, and what scraps remained were scoffed up by the giant. After this, he came to his wheelbarrow and brought forth a large leather container. He upended this over his mouth, gulped down a good measure of whatever liquor it contained, then, without preparing any sort of bed, flopped down upon the ground, rolled over onto his back and added his snores to those of the teamster.

The next morning the giant was gone, but the teamster accompanied the expedition as the native attack had unsettled him. He swore over and over again to any within earshot that he had no intention of being stuck like some pig and ending up on a spit. 'I like a bit of roast pork meself,' he growled at Sergeant Barron, whom he was cultivating with a bottle of superior whisky, 'but I hesitates to be pork meself.'

'They don't eat people,' Barron scoffed.

'Ye never can tell what they eat until ye are what they eat,' the teamster retorted.

'Well, you'd better watch out for my boys,' laughed the sergeant. 'They're just out of the woods and they might have their eyes on you. You've got a bit of meat on your bones too,' he added, poking him in the gut.

'No bloody joking matter, mate,' the man replied, pulling out a huge pistol. 'See this? If one of yer black buggers, constable or not, comes near me with a hungry gleam in his eye, that'll be the end of him. Aye, it will be.'

'And the end of you too,' Barron stated flatly. 'My boys are civilised enough to enjoy a good dance at the end of a rope and if you let off that thing in their direction, that's what it'll be, for the governor enjoys a hanging more than a flogging.' And with that he stamped off to get the expedition underway.

The journey continued on without incident, except a horse was found to have suffered a loss of blood from a wound inflicted by an unknown animal. Russian Jack continued at his own pace. The expedition passed him on the track but by nightfall he had caught up with them. They grew tired of sharing their provisions with him, but when they shot the horse (too weak from loss of blood to travel), he stayed behind to carve some steaks from it. 'Waste not, want bloody not,' he declared, as he cut the meat into strips, put them on the end of sticks and smoked them over a fire. This took the best part of a day and so there was no passing of

Russian Jack that day nor his arrival in camp that night; before he caught up, they were at Yillarn.

The diggings sprawled across the wide bed of an ancient stream that had long since dried out, though a few deep wells had been dug down to brackish water. So many men had arrived there that a veritable tent city had sprung up and there was scarcely a spot which had not been claimed. At last, they found a camping site on what had been the bank of the stream. It was pitted with shallow holes, for the fossickers had tried their luck there, before deciding that any alluvial gold would lie in the bed rather than on the banks. This, they had carved up into small mining plots of approximately fifty feet by fifty feet. As yet there was no system of registering claims and a man took what he might hold and work. All disputes were settled by a rough court of miners.

The teamster was a mine of information about the diggings and regaled Sergeant Barron and Sir George with stories whenever he could. 'There's not much thieving of a man's belongings,' he told them. 'Of course some goes on, and when the bloke is caught he's given short shrift. There was this blighter who was caught pilfering in a tent while the owner was away working his claim. When something like this happens a tin dish is beaten and the fossickers come all together. Well, he had been caught red-handed and they told him to get out and not come back again. He got out and no one's ever seen him again. It happens out here like that. They ups and disappears.

'Of course,' he went on, 'sometimes it happens that a bloke comes across a large slug of gold when his mates are not about. There's always the temptation to pocket it. Well, there was this bloke who shared a claim with two others. It's easier that way, what with the scarcity of water. Ye have to dry blow the dirt and this means ye need someone to throw it up while others shake the sieve below. Two or three pairs of hands make for lighter work, eh? Well, back to these blokes, two of them go for tucker, leave their mate behind to look after things. Get back and they ask him, "Found anything?" "Not a trace." They believe him, but ye can't find gold without it getting known and the bloke on the next piece of dirt came up to them and said: "Nice size piece of metal he found the other day." "Errh, yes," they reply, trying not to let on that they had been diddled, but their faces gave them away. Still, he was their mate and true blue. "No one's true blue when a big slug of gold is weighing down his hand," the fellow said. "You just ask him and if he denies it, beat the dish and we'll roll up and sort out the matter." Well, they put the word to their mate, who looked as guilty as they were told he was. Finding that the game was up, he at last said (though his look showed he lied) that he had been keeping it as a surprise for them. Couldn't he have thought of something better? Ye get me in that situation and on with the blarney I'd be till I was as green as Ireland. Well, the upshot was that the slug was divided between the three of them and the thieving bloke was gone by daylight. Never been seen since. Maybe the blacks got him; maybe someone else got him. Gold does that to blokes, you know.'

'Well, that may be the justice here now,' retorted Sergeant Barron, an upholder of the Queen's law in the colony, 'but as soon as I get my orders, there'll be proper law and order here. You can't just have blokes disappearing and gold being stolen and all that. You need proper rules and regulations. In no time at all, there'll be murderings going on. Anarchy, like the Frenchies had in their so-called revolution, until a soldier came along to put a stop to it.'

'Well, not if they can help it,' the teamster replied. 'There's enough rope; but some things are better left unsaid, eh?'

'Or to the hangman!'

'But you fellows must keep order as you see fit,' enjoined Sir George, 'for Sergeant Barron and his troopers are the escort for my expedition and are under strict orders. Let the fossickers deal with things in their own rough way. It won't last that long. Just be thankful that there are no convicts in this colony, or thieving would be a daily occurrence, not to mention murder and mayhem.'

'Thank the Lord for that,' the teamster replied, 'and may the colony remain free of such rogues and vagabonds. We're all free settlers here, not a mark of the leg iron on any one of us,' he said, squinting down at his own ankle.

This conversation had taken place on the last night before the diggings were reached. Now Sir George was looking down at the dusty scene in which men laboured like ants, producing a pall of dust which hung in the air like a heavy fog. As he stared from the bank he could see how all of the ground over the wide dry bed had been taken up. If he ever decided to try his luck at prospecting, he would have to be in on a new strike; but then, with his inside information, what need had he of new strikes? His mission and the native guide were leading him to where the first piece of gold ore had been found and where there was, according to the native, more; much, much more. Of course, experience had taught him that often little credence could be placed on the word of savages; but that was only when they thought you wanted a specific answer. Well, he hadn't. But if nothing came of it, he might finance a few of the miners and let them do his work for him. With the surface gold almost gone here, it was only a matter of time before mining companies were established, and that would be what to get in on. Well, that might be the future if his expedition did not pan out as supposed. This evening, he would visit Paddy's grog shop and keep his ears open.

CHAPTER FOUR

'I'm Russian Jack and I've been on the road for a month and my supply of grog ran out at the end of the first week. I'm raring to wet my whistle and get the old throat clear of that dust that cakes it so. Bloody desert and that bloody mate, for leaving me to go it alone.'

The giant flung a pound note at Paddy. He was tossed a bottle of rotgut whisky in return, which he upended over his mouth before passing it to one of the men who had not found enough colour to keep him thirst-free. The large tent was filled with diggers, who clustered before the rough planks of the bar, or sat and squatted on the floor or on forms consisting of planks of wood on top of logs. There was no breeze, not even a flutter at the canvas, and the men, many of whom were smoking, filled the space with an effluvium made up of tobacco fumes and body odours, for there was not enough water for drinking, let alone bathing. Still, the grog flowed freely. Those who had struck paydirt bragged about it, or were secretive until the liquor loosened their tongues and their pockets.

'Another, Paddy, and this one's all for meself,' the Russian called, banging another note onto the counter. 'There! But next time, it'll be gold.

'Ah, that's good, and now that dark coot has put an end to his yarn about white things that go bump in the night and suck the blood from unsuspecting blackfellows, I'll give you a tale of suchlike too. Well, in Russia, there's things called Eretiks, and to get rid of them you must drive an aspen stake into their back and through to the heart. Has to be the back door though, and after you've done that, burn the body till only ashes remains. That gets rid of them and for ever. Well, you might be thinking, how does this bloke know about such things? Don't say it out loud though, 'cause me fist is a bit heavy and when it hits yer jaw ... Well, I know about it 'cause I had me a mate, a soldier in the Czar's army, who fought against whoever there was to fight against, Tartars and suchlike. He did his share of the killing, got a bit of a wound and came home on furlough.

'What was the name of his town? Nicolsk, I think it was. Well, he got there, goes into the inn and gets to talking with this bloke, just an ordinary sort of blighter, and they have a few and maybe more, for we Russians know how to put it away. That's why we have big bellies, need the space to hold it all. Well, this mate of mine, Alexi, had come back for a wedding and he turns to his new friend and says: "Relatives hitching up, come along and wet their future life together. The more the merrier and all that." Well, with his mate in tow, he gets to the house. And while my soldier mate got stuck into the grog, the Eretik, for that was what he was, got stuck into the bride and groom.

'He began to drain their life blood and Alexi saw this and was most upset. "Can't do that, not on their wedding day, they won't have the strength later on, and there's the matter of the bloody towel to consider."

'"Can't I? But I am," declared the Eretik in a voice as deep as a grave. But, yer know, for some reason – well, I suppose it's hard for an Eretik to make friends, what with his nasty habits – he had taken a liking to Alexi. He hesitated in his blood collecting (he had taken a sip or two and was getting more to have at his leisure) and they got to yarning. He must have been a pretty stupid bloodsucker for he let on to Alexi how to put an end to such creatures as himself.

'The upshot was that he was chased out of that house with me mate waving an aspen stake over his head. Alexi'd had a bit to drink and missed his swing, though he knocked from the monster's hand the two vials in which he was collecting the life blood. He caught 'em as they fell, then poured the blood back into the wounds the Eretik had made in the newly weds – who perked up to do the needful that night.

'The guests went after the bloodsucker. That thing had even told me mate where his body lay, and they got to the cemetery, dug up the body, pounded that aspen stake through his back, burnt the corpse and buried the ashes at the crossways so that, if he still survived that, he would be hung there like on a cross. Ashes to ashes, eh, and the devil was no more.

'And that's what me mate, Alexi, told me on a night like this with the grog flowing freely down our throats just as now. Well, a yarn must end as must good times. Paddy, another one for the road. That blighter's hiding out from me, but I'll find him, for it's on the track tomorrow; though no bloody shank's pony this time. Horse and dray, mate, horse and dray. Hey, better give that one a mate. I'll need a nightcap and in the morning an eye-opener. Got me a flask to fill later too. That's for the track ...'

Clutching a bottle in each hand, the giant got to his feet, swaying from side to side. He lurched forward and out into the night, brushing past Sir George, who was standing before the grog shop.

The knight put a smile on his face and went to the seat that the Russian had just vacated. 'Evening, men,' he called out. He noticed a ragged native sitting in a corner. 'You boy, what are you doing here? Why aren't you with your tribe?' he asked. He was puzzled for there seemed to be something familiar about the boy, but then he thrust the thought aside as unimportant.

There was; for not only was the boy the knight's son, George, but Mrs Fraser's dog in his human form. He was a regular mix: the result of one of Sir George's lusty attacks on a native woman under his care; and under the spell of the woman who treated him as a pet to be fondled and patted. Sir George shifted his attention easily, for the event had happened long ago and he had put such things out of mind. But his son, George, longed for his father's recognition and stared at the knight with large, dark, wet eyes in which the faithfulness of the animal glowed. His gaze was ignored, as he had been the time past when he had tried to get through to his father after meeting him on the coast. He sighed and even gave a doggish whine; but then remembered his mistress who was good to him, and he thought of her hand on him and felt the need to be with her.

'Don't worry about that fellow,' Paddy said. 'He's not all black. One of those mixed ones and he's as much right to be in here as you have. He paid for his welcome with a story that rivalled that Russian bloke's and he didn't even accept a drink for it, though I wish he had a coin or two to shout a round for the chaps,' he hinted to the toff.

'Sir,' Sir George began ominously, his voice rising towards a harangue; then he thought better of it, though he did introduce himself and emphasised the importance of his mission in saving such natives from lives of utter degradation. Even these words made the men yawn and start up conversations among themselves, while the native who had been the occasion for the words got to his feet and wandered from the tent. Sir George, having gained the attention of the diggers and quickly lost it, now regained it by calling for drinks all round.

'And how is the precious metal on this field?' he asked, hiding his eagerness, as those who were most interested in the topic often sought to do. The men with gold uttermost in their minds knew that everyone was after it. They played the new chum along.

'Just about played out, mate, if you ask me,' a grizzled old timer spoke up. 'Been here from the first find and now the findings are just about gone. If yer after gold, try further east. Not a rush yet, just a trickle to a place called Skull's Flat. That'll be the place to head, mark my words; though, mate, it's bad news, as those who go there find out. Yer know how it got its name?'

'Rich pickings, if you've got the nerve,' another man broke in. 'But them skulls, they spooks a lot. Some says evil lurks there, mate, evil as black as the Devil and those poor blighters who have been caught. Well, at night there's the clink of stones in a tin dish as, doomed for ever more, they toss the dirt up and down, up and down, to separate out the metal.

Those skulls, the remains of poor fossickers. Three blokes who came to the Devil's playground. Hot and desolate as hell. No water, no nothing, but plenty of sun and dust stirred up to race about like devils in a dance. Well, they camped there at a dried-up waterhole which was marked by the skeleton of a dead tree like an upside-down cross. They found it, mate, the mother lode. Enough for all. But one of them, a big black Irishman by the name of Sean, well, he got the fever. He waited until the night and there came the Devil to put the axe in his hand. His mates were sleeping. Thud, thud went that axe. He hacked off their heads and next morning boiled them up till the flesh fell away. He stuck a skull on the ends of two branches of that dead tree and in the eye sockets he placed gleaming nuggets. And, yer know what then? The grub was all gone and so he lived on the bodies of his mates. Ate 'em all up. He finished them off and by then he was all out of his head, a regular Bedlamite you might say. But it was the Devil finishing him off and soon his body lay beside the skeletons of his mates. True as there's a God above and a Devil below, for others have gone and saw those skulls and tried for the gold and ended up with their bodies drying out. Evil, mate, the Devil and those skulls and that growing heap of bones.'

'Arrh, come off it,' another spoke up. 'Thirst, that's what got them, and after that the dingoes. Those wild dogs came, gnawed on their bones and heaped them up like that. There's gold there, gold for the picking. We'll all be there soon – bones or skulls, or even the Devil at his play, nothing will keep us away.'

'Yeah, mate,' the grizzled old timer butted in. 'Go and dance with the Devil.'

'The Devil may be there, he's all over this country anyway, and I'd give him my soul for a bag or two of gold.'

'Fellows, Satan is no laughing matter, and as for selling your souls ...' Sir George began, then changed his mind. 'There must be other likely places; though, as I've said, I'm on a mission of mercy and succour. Still ...'

'So are we, mate,' the old timer replied. 'Lord have mercy and keep the gold coming.' Then he was shouted down as Sir George ordered another round of drinks.

'Don't listen to him or any other of these cadgers,' a man yelled in Sir George's ear, rum fumes almost intoxicating the knight. 'That old blighter will tell you this and that and even offer to guide you for a price. He's on the lookout for someone to stake him, though he hasn't found even a trace of colour. To hear him talk he's the one who discovered the metal here.'

'I was only about to tell him of Kalipa,' the old timer said grievously.

'Our El Dorado, our Promised Land, where the ground is covered by nuggets and there's not the need of dry blowing. Christ, I hate those shakers. How weary my arms get, and if you're not careful the gold dust passes through with the dirt. We need water, lots and lots of it, to wash away the dirt and leave that gold shining in the bottom of our pans. El Dorado, mate, the Promised Land; and what's more, it has the precious fluid. A big soak, naw a lake filled with sweet water; but it's not needed when you can just go and pick up a slug or two or a thousand. Just for the picking, just for the picking. It's what I dream about, splashing in that water while I toss up the nuggets.'

'Yeah, dreams,' exclaimed the drunk, trying for another drink by wrapping an arm about the knight's shoulders. 'Nothing like a fairy tale to ease the night along. But like all fairy tales, there's wicked ogres, so why not tell him about the blacks? If he wants blackfellows, he'll find them there; though not the gold, if that's what he's after.'

'I might just go there,' agreed Sir George.

'Savages, downright bloodthirsty savages,' another prospector broke in. 'Scalp you even before they stick you with their godawful spears. You find your blacks there, mate, and nothing else but dust and stones. Yeah, and yer know what that heathen name means?'

'Not El Dorado,' Sir George replied sardonically. He knew that savages were more often timid than aggressive.

'Kalipa, the Killing Field,' the old timer said, giving an exaggerated shudder.

'Oh, Kalipa,' Sir George repeated. 'Killing Fields, eh?' It was where Monaitch had told him he had picked up that piece of gold-bearing ore which had sparked this rush. Thank God, it was still safe from these fossickers.

'Yes, Kalipa,' the drunk slurred. To get the man to remove his arm, Sir George ordered another round of drinks.

'Kalipa, El Dorado,' the old fellow yelped from the bar, unable to hide the grin that split his face to reveal the shattered remains of his teeth.

'Thank you, gentlemen,' the knight replied. 'Now, let us forget the barren Kalipa and drink to this field and to your health and, hopefully, wealth.'

'But not at Kalipa,' the men chorused, breaking into guffaws before raising their mugs.

CHAPTER FIVE

Sir George would not have expected to find a veritable forest in this harsh arid land where even the sweat dried up as soon as it appeared. He had thought that it would be a relatively easy matter to navigate across the plain by dead reckoning, but this was soon in doubt when Kalipa was not to be found on the chart which had been plotted by the Bailey expedition. Without this aid, Sir George was forced to rely on the God-fearing Monaitch who, eschewing all forms of paganism, said that he trusted that the Lord would guide him to their destination. In spite of this absolute reliance, he still followed certain natural signs which on occasion he pointed out to Sir George, who was thankful for them, for there seemed to be lodestone about and his compass swung crazily whenever he tried to consult it to get his bearings. Now they had come to a wide belt of what Monaitch informed him were mallee trees. They completely blocked up the land so that the expedition had to follow the bed of an ancient stream which, though sand, was baked hard and solid enough to endure the wheels of their carts.

Where once they had had the sight of the wide flat land extending from horizon to horizon, they now had the spindly trunks of the dwarf trees hemming them in on all sides. This induced a feeling of claustrophobia, which Sir George, remembering the dank forests of the south island, thrust away by lustily singing hymns which he hoped the native troopers would pick up, since music was the universal language. Sergeant Barron had been forced to attend many a church parade and, also feeling oppressed by the spindly forest through which they meandered, sang along in quite a nice baritone. Their combined voices sank into the trees and the branches, and leaves fluttered as small birds fled from the racket.

'Lead, kindly Light, amid the encircling gloom,
Lead Thou me on;
The night is dark, and I am far from home.
Keep Thou my feet; I do not ask to see
The distant scene; one step enough for me ...'

The words might have driven Mrs Fraser into a frenzy, but her day-induced lassitude did not make for strong emotions. All she did was put her hands over her ears while leaning back in the swaying bughi, which ran smoothly on the hard sand, and let her mind drift about with thoughts of prey, for she was ravenous. Not wishing to alarm the others by seeking their blood, she had taken to drinking that of the horses – much like a Cossack – and this led her to thoughts of the giant Russian and how she would have liked to sample him, even though she did not like her drink to be flavoured with rum or whisky. Well, she sighed as she stared through her veil at the constricting landscape, who knew what prey might be found at the end of the journey. If natives there were, they would serve her well, for she enjoyed their blood uncontaminated by civilisation's vices and Christian sourness.

Her thoughts were disturbed by Monaitch, who was leading the expedition on horseback. He wheeled his jaded mount about and came to Sir George. He said nothing until the verse of the hymn had finished, then pointed down at the ground. The knight followed his finger and saw to his dismay the faint twin marks of a wheeled vehicle.

'White fellow come this way, recently,' Monaitch said, gesturing ahead at the remains of a campfire. A cast-off bottle shone in the sunlight.

'How many fellows?' asked Sir George, hoping against hope that their destination had not become the goal of fossickers.

'Only one, two.'

'Well, this vacant land beckons those with gold fever as much as it beckons us on our Christian journey of mercy,' he declared, and not being able to do anything about it, lifted his voice and sang the last verse of the hymn:

'So long Thou power hath blest me, sure it still will lead me on,
O'er moor and fen, o'er crag and torrent, till the night is gone;
And with the morn those angel faces smile,
Which I have loved long since, and lost awhile.'

'Amen,' Amelia whispered sardonically, listlessly poking her foot into the dog's stomach.

'Amen, amen,' Monaitch replied enthusiastically.

'Amen,' Sir George muttered, then again with more feeling as he saw that the dwarf forest was losing its grip upon the land. Soon they were out of it and onto a plain covered with tussocks of grass which would provide forage for the horses.

Sir George was staring directly at the featureless horizon when there came a vision splendid. There in the sky but upside down was a pool of water with a grove of small white-trunked, fuzzy-topped trees to one side and a shallow wadi on the other. It was an oasis.

Monaitch exclaimed: 'A sign, a sign. That is Kalipa!'

'Yes, yes,' the knight replied, staring at the phantom scene, amazed at how detailed it was, even to the extent that he could see two figures, white men, dressed in corduroy and checked shirts. They were bent over something which, as they scratched at it, suddenly gave out a beam of golden light. He watched as the two men began an ungainly dance. 'They have found my gold,' he exclaimed, before recovering to muter: 'They must be dislodged and I must find a means to do so. Look, there are natives, filling their skinbags at the pool.'

'I declare that it is the giant Russian.' Mrs Fraser suddenly spoke up, her hand tightening about the loose skin at the dingo's neck. 'And it appears that they have found a slug of gold.'

'They have indeed,' Sir George said dryly, 'and by rights it should have been mine and, and ... It was my purpose to build a mission in that very place and bring those children of nature you see there to the light. That golden light you saw was but His light shining out over those who live in darkness. This is no mirage, but a vision of my future work that will make a thriving settlement there.' And he began another hymn:

> 'Can we, whose souls are lighted
> With wisdom from on high,
> Can we to men benighted
> The lamp of life deny?
> Salvation! oh, salvation!
> The joyful sound proclaim,
> Till each remotest nation
> Has learn'd Messiah's name.'

'Hallelujah,' shouted Monaitch. 'Hallelujah!'

'And he who holds the land, holds the gold,' observed the woman, her voice almost a whisper. Her pet raised its head, pricked up its ears, then, as if deciding that it had had enough singing for the day, jumped down and into the spindly forest to find what it could in the way of food.

'For God's work, for God's work,' the knight declared, then lapsed into silence as he thought over how he might effect the transfer of the land into his own name.

Two days later they reached the oasis. Their arrival was ignored by the two prospectors, who stopped digging where they had been and shifted to another spot. The expedition set up camp away from the wadi and near the trees which were too low to camp under. By evening, Sir George had everything arranged to his satisfaction and even Sergeant Barron had stopped his shouted commands. Sir George thought of taking Mrs Fraser over to meet the prospectors but decided against it; instead he took along two bottles of his precious brandy, which he had kept in his box of goodies. These, he hoped, would ensure his welcome and put the two men at their ease. The dingo watched him go, then slunk after him.

Russian Jack scowled when he saw the man coming, but then his eyes went to the bottles and he gave a welcoming grin. Soon he was upending a bottle over his gulping mouth while Sir George smiled in amusement and derision, and sorrow, for it was good brandy. He next turned his attention to the Russian's mate. An ungainly man with a rather prominent nose and sloping forehead beneath thatch-like hair. The man seemed familiar and was. Sir George gave a gasp. It was his son, Sonny, who had betrayed his father's trust when he had been left in charge of the mission on the island and had disappeared without a trace, the schooner along with him.

'Sonny, Sonny,' the knight called. 'Here is your father and he is here to call you to account. I left you in charge of my life's work and what did you do but desert your post as soon as I made myself absent. Where is my schooner?'

'I-I-I ...' stuttered a startled Sonny. The last thing he had expected was for his father to find him here; but he should have known that he could never escape him. He was like a bad penny, always turning up.

Under his father's stern gaze, the hobbledehoy, though he was edging thirty, tugged at his dusty lank hair, felt the bald spot at the crown, buttoned up his shirt which he had left undone, then tugged up his trousers.

'Sonny, Sonny, just look at yourself,' intoned Sir George. 'You might once have made something of yourself, and now what are you but some dishevelled tramp adrift in a wilderness of his own devising. I had high hopes for you. A minister of religion succouring those around him. How sad to see you as you are.' He shook his head sorrowfully and lapsed into silence, as if the sight of his son had overpowered his feelings. But in truth the vision splendid was still in his mind, together with the knowledge that he always had been able to control his dolt of a son, especially through his mother, whom the boy had always loved in a dependence which rankled with his father. Definitely like mother like son, Sir George thought as he remembered his dead wife. She had expended too much affection on the boy; the result of which was the weakling that slouched before him.

'Your mother called for you with her dying breath, but you were not there,' Sir George said sadly. 'I ordered a special boat to hurry you to her, but the mission was deserted and you were not to be found, and nor were your charges. Sonny, Sonny, you disappointed me and hurt your mother and myself as deeply as a son can his parents.'

'I-I-I-' began the son, but his father lifted a hand to stop him.

'Still, I am a Christian and thus turn the other cheek and forgive you. You are here and I am here: the reunion of a father and a son is a matter of rejoicing. Find some vessels so that we may drink to the coming together of those who have been forced apart, though it has not been through adversity but rather through a son's wilfulness. I expect you wrecked my schooner. No matter, no matter, it was the government's. It was reported to have floundered in the big storm that struck the islands. An act of Providence, for you might have been on a charge of piracy. Stealing a vessel is a hanging matter, son; but I protected you as always.'

'I-I-I-' said Sonny.

'No matter, you are forgiven and we shall drink to it and our reunion.'

Sir George filled one of the pannikins his son brought, then added three fingerfuls to his own. He glanced across at the Russian, who was nursing his bottle and seemed to have sunk into a daze. This suited Sir George's purposes, for what he wanted he wanted without the Russian's knowledge. He was heartened when his son quickly drained his pannikin. He refilled it, before squatting beside him and conversing about Sonny's mother and how she had died. He had the boy-man almost snivelling by the time he had finished. He replenished his mug whilst saying: 'It is hard for a son to lose his mother and harder still when that son was not there to hold her hand for a last time. Still, with her dying breath she forgave you, and then when I found that you had deserted your post, I too forgave you. The schooner was old and unseaworthy anyway. You are absolved.'

He glanced at the Russian who had fallen asleep and then changed the topic. 'Sonny, what do you do here in this wilderness? I never expected to find you here. Perhaps you should return with me. There is nothing here except rocks and sand, and the blacks who are my reason for being here.'

'All right here,' his son retorted, his strength coming from the huge slug of gold and the many smaller ones he and Russian Jack had picked up on the first day of their arrival. 'No, no, this is the place for me, and how can I desert a mate. Together we came and when he goes so shall I. It is-is-is-' He broke off and his father filled his mug again, then added a thimbleful of liquor to his own.

Sir George sipped slowly, savouring the aroma of the good brandy, sad that he had had to use two full bottles: one to pacify a fellow who drank alcohol as if it was water and another on a son who was going the same way as his companion.

Sir George watched him now as, not even hesitating a moment to enjoy the taste of the brandy, Sonny tossed off half a mug. He stared away from the sight and into the darkness as he said: 'No matter, you shall come back with me.'

'Shan't,' declared the drunken man. 'Shan't until I'm good and ready. There are bags of the stuff here and when we have filled up all that the dray can carry, then I shall go, but not till then and it'll be with my mate too.'

'Do you mean gold, son?' asked his father in a low voice.

'Yes, and oodles and oodles of it,' Sonny whispered fiercely, as if someone might hear him. 'Oodles and oodles and I shall be able to buy what I want.'

'That much, Sonny?'

'That much and more. Oodles and oodles, I've said, and it's all ours – ours, and no one shall take it away from me. Not even you, and I shall stay here until I am good and ready. Not like that other time when you and Mum went away and left me all alone with a mob of savages who stole that schooner. Well, I'll just buy another and better one for you, then we'll be square ...'

He fell into a scowling silence. His father sipped at his brandy and waited.

Sonny relived that day when he had been left in charge of the mission. He had given out the rations, then, not having anything else to do, had found the rum and begun drinking. He had intended to have only a few swallows to get over the feeling of being abandoned, but as the day wore on, he'd continued drinking. Finally, he staggered from his father's house to find the mission deserted of even the blacks. He lurched towards the chapel, calling out: 'Ludjee, Ludjee, where you gotten to, eh? Jangamuttuk, Jangamuttuk, rations, rations. No show, no gettee, eh!'

He began sobbing as he sank into the awful depression of that final scene. He had fallen in the doorway of the chapel, though without spilling his drink. He had taken a long swallow and then sobbed into the desolation. Not a single person to help him and it was worse when he pulled himself together enough to focus his eyes on the beach where the schooner had been anchored. It had gone; but this lessened his alarm, for it meant that the African, Wadawaka, had taken all the natives with him when he moved it to a more sheltered bay. It had been impossible to imagine that Wadawaka and the savages had stolen the schooner and sailed off, leaving him stranded on a deserted island. It still rankled. 'They hated me,' he told his father, wiping away his tears and finishing off his mug of brandy. 'They hated me and when you left, they left.'

'Sonny, Sonny, I have forgiven you, and you should have been firm with them. I came on the relief boat for you. My poor mission without inhabitants. I searched without success. Why, I even offered a reward for news of your whereabouts. It was a sad day indeed when I felt I had lost my son and heir.' Sir George wiped an imaginary tear from his eye, before adding: 'But I have found you and that is enough, and what is more, you have made good as I always knew you would. Gold, you have found gold and will be rich.'

'A great big nugget, bigger than I've ever imagined, and pure through and through.'

'But Sonny, perhaps you are exaggerating, it may be merely iron pyrites. The red of the soil denotes iron and my compass has drifted far from the north.'

'No, gold, gold. Russian Jack knows gold and it is ours.'

'Well, perhaps you could show it to me. I don't know whether to believe you or not.'

'Show it to you! It's hidden, dug into the ground under a stone. We'll cache all that we find there. This place is El Dorado and we are the first on the strike.'

'And where is this hole, Sonny?'

'Won't tell you. Secret!'

'But how can I believe you, if I don't see this slug· of gold with my own eyes?'

'Just have to believe me. Secret, it is. Russian Jack wouldn't like it. He says keep it hidden, especially from you lot.'

'Sonny, the Lord and I do not like liars, nor did your mother –'

'Not lying, not lying. Come, I'll show you whether I'm lying or not.' He staggered to his feet and tripped over the comatose Russian, who gave a groan followed by an oath before lapsing back into unconsciousness. Sonny wrenched the bottle from his mate's arms, took a long swallow, then replaced it. 'Keep it safe for me,' he slurred as he tried to get back onto his feet. Sir George helped him up and he went lurching towards the wadi which was directly in front of the camp, slid down the bank and fell at a large rock. It was as far as he could go and soon he began to snore.

Sir George stared down at his son, then bent down and got him under his arms and dragged him towards the bank. It was hard going for a man past sixty and he might not have succeeded had not a voice spoken beside him: 'What's wrong with him?'

'Drunk,' Sir George said as he recognised the voice. 'I want to get him back to his camp.'

'Well, let me help,' replied Mrs Fraser. She calmly lifted the man and half slung him up to the top of the bank. 'Now, you take his legs and I'll take his feet and soon he'll be safely tucked into what serves him for a bed.'

This was soon done and Sir George attempted to get rid of the woman so that he might go and seek out the buried treasure. He feigned going back to his tent, but she stayed with him.

'There is supposed to be lots of gold here,' she said.

'Perhaps, but I have not seen any,' Sir George replied. 'What I am interested in and what concerns me is the plight of the indigenous inhabitants. Why, if these two prospectors have reached here, how many of their fellows will follow them and what will happen to the poor natives when the whole area is overflowing with the rascals? They need a place of refuge. And one with a constant supply of water so that they might plant crops and grow vegetables.'

'This is the very place for a mission, as you yourself declared when that mirage appeared in the sky. It was a sign,' Amelia stated. 'Surely, this piece of land far from any settlement is of little value and the governor will grant it to you for such a worthy cause.'

'But these fossickers are spreading out like a plague of locusts and we must move fast if we are to get the land; but how can I when there are so many miles between us and the town?'

'Sergeant Barron has an eye for the ladies and I believe that I could persuade him to send one of his troopers. Write the letter and I shall see that it is as quickly received as if it were sent by wire.'

'I must pray for guidance in this matter. Now, if you will leave me, I will decide on it.'

While they had been conversing, Mrs Fraser had deftly turned their steps to the top of the wadi. Her pet trotted on past her and went down into the gully. She watched as he went along the bottom to sniff at a large flat stone. She left the knight's side and followed her dog to the whitish stone that shone in the starlight. Perforce, Sir George came puffing after her.

'My dingo has tracked them to this stone. Perhaps those two have found gold and hidden it here,' she murmured. 'If such is the case, the urgency of having this area declared mission land is doubled. If the land is made private, the prospectors can be barred from it.'

Sir George huffed and puffed. He had no intention of taking anyone, especially this woman, into his confidence. 'My single concern is for the future wellbeing of the natives,' he declared. 'Gold or no gold, it is the perfect place for a ration depot to concentrate the natives so that they may be encouraged to settle. O Lord, give unto your servant this piece of land so that he may further your work in this wilderness bereft of your light.'

'Yes, Sir George,' observed Amelia tartly. 'Enough of hypocrisy, both gold and savages can be gleaned from this land. Look, my dear doggy is trying to push aside the slab all by himself. What could be under it, I wonder?'

She stooped and shoved aside the flat boulder. Below it was a cavity which held a fragment of what seemed to be rock, and other pieces the size of bullets. Sir George, in trepidation, bent down and felt the large piece. It was covered with curlicues like the fleece of a sheep. He held it up – not without some effort, for it was heavy – to his face. Where the surface had been scraped it gleamed in the starlight with a glow which he knew was the precious metal. 'Gold, gold,' he whispered harshly. 'We have found gold.'

'It is not ours, but theirs, or even the dog's by right of discovery,' observed the woman sardonically.

'We shall see, we shall see,' Sir George grunted in a passion, 'for if I have the land then I have the gold and these two are mere trespassers.'

'But do not forget the natives,' Mrs Fraser replied with an amused note in her voice. 'It is their land morally and what is here is theirs.'

'Of course, I never forget the natives,' the knight replied. 'I shall merely be a custodian and hold both land and gold for their good. Now I must cover over this hoard. They must not know that their secret is out. Sonny I can deal with; but that Russian, he is a brute and a ruffian.'

'He is indeed a giant of a man; but first you must get the land and after that he can – well, he can be expelled, or removed. If such wealth is to be gained, risks must be taken.'

'Yes, yes, and now that you are in the secret, that letter must quickly be written, well sealed and sent off. See what you can do with the sergeant and if all goes well it shall be on its way tomorrow.'

'Or tomorrow night,' the woman observed. Calling her dingo to her, she left Sir George, her black clad figure merging into the darkness as she disappeared over the bank. When she was gone, the knight uncovered the treasure trove again and raised the huge nugget high so that the light of the stars glinted off it. He put it to one side and dipped his hand into the hole where he felt the many small pellets. He clutched one to his mouth and bit down.

'Solid gold,' he exclaimed, 'and it is worth any effect to make it all mine.'

CHAPTER SIX

Next morning a group of natives had appeared from the desert to stop near the waterhole. When they found it inhabited by Sir George and his party, they camped anyway, but not too near. They lit their fires across the gully and in the afternoon the women came with wooden dishes for water. Not a man showed himself, but Sir George knew that when the natives found themselves in a situation which they could not fathom, they sent the women ahead to scout out the land, or in this case to get water, while they skulked behind ready to attack.

He issued strict orders that the natives be left alone until he had established a friendly contact with them. This was easier said than done, for after the women had gotten water, some returned to spy out the camp. Like black nude statues they stood still and eyed the scene about them with living eyes. Sir George, who knew a good illustration when he saw one, had Mrs Fraser sketch them, which she did until the sun streaked red over the land and they went back to the camp.

The sun sank and the welcome darkness settled. It was time for Amelia to be off. She thought about taking Dog with her, but decided against it as he might fly off by himself and she would have to seek him out. She called him into the tent and eased their separation before she departed, telling him that she would be gone only a night, or maybe two, she amended, and he must fend for himself. He whined and licked her hand, but she refused to take him. Now she divested herself of her clothing, packed it away into her chest, then, transforming into a bat, she fluttered up into the sky and landed just beyond the native camp.

She would feed first and here she would find her meal. Resuming her human shape, a pale thing of the night, she crept around the camp to come across a girl squatting in the sand. She called to her softly, but the infant sprang to her feet and was already running when the woman pounced. Holding the squirming child in her arms, Amelia pressed the tiny face against her breasts until the girl quietened enough for her to adjust her grip. One hand went over the child's mouth to stop any screams as she bent over the neck vein and sank in her fangs. The blood was fresh and young and she quickly drained the child, then tossed the tiny corpse away. Refreshed and invigorated, she became Bat and darted off to the southwest.

It was towards midnight when she swooped towards a small dainty tree which grew in solitude on the desolate plain. She slowed as she neared, ready to take a needed rest, for the letter was ungainly in her claws. As she fluttered down, there came a movement of air that alerted her. Huge wings beat behind her. Instantly she sought refuge in the tree, waiting to see what it might be. A large grey mass, with wings dotted with white spots shining in the starlight, flew towards her, then fell to the ground with a plop before reaching the tree. She tried to hear what it was up to, but there was no longer the movement of air which had alerted her and her sensitive ears could not locate it. Uneasily she hung there, then darted into the air to flee. As she did so, she heard the flapping of great wings. The monster was after her. She sped on, but it came steadily nearer. Too close! She swirled, came up and over the thing and dived down. A huge owl, but not so big that if she managed to get her claws into the bird and then transformed, her weight would drag it to the ground. All the while she would be ripping at its throat. The thought came: what would owl's blood taste like? It was then that she brushed past the bird and found that the letter was still in her claws.

She could not drop it to attack, and with it would find it difficult to fend him off. Then she found her situation worse, for the monster had in its mouth one of those shamanic crystals which had hurt her before, when she had been with the natives. A red beam of light flashed out, barely missing her. She darted aside from another and another. The letter was impeding her movements, but she was loath to release it. She fled towards the ground, to a blow hole in the desert floor in which she could take refuge.

Over it, she folded her wings, letting herself fall through into subterranean darkness. Abruptly, she twisted up to a ledge just inside the hole. She put the letter down, transformed, then waited to get the monster if he ventured inside. Just let him come in, just! Owl blood. She licked her lips.

She strained her ears, but there was no sound from without. Wait, there ... She transformed into Bat so that she could use her superior senses. Bare feet padding stealthily towards the hole.

She switched back, picked up a sharp rock and watched as slowly and carefully a head appeared, blocking out some of the stars. A human head, and she flung the rock up at it. There was a screech and there was the huge head of the owl, its savage eyes glaring down at her. How she could battle this thing, especially when the crystal glowed in its mouth – blue, this time. Taking up the letter, she fell off the ledge and down into the hole. She fell and fell, but the monster did not come after her.

Sir George Augustus had done all that could be done for the time being and was now nervously prowling about the oasis. On such occasions, and there had been a few, he took recourse in his favourite picture. A large work painted by a convict on the south island. The oil depicted his greatest triumph, which he had used to elevate himself beyond his class. He smiled as he remembered how he used to drop his aitches. 'A long time ago now,' he murmured as he unrolled the large canvas. There he stood in the prime of his manhood: not a warrior, but a saviour of bodies and souls. Severe in clerical black, though not unsmiling, he stretched out a hand to, to – why, to that old rascal, Jangamuttuk, who gazed back at him in thanksgiving. He wondered what had happened to the old fellow. The artist had depicted Sir George with his left hand upraised as if in a blessing, or a calling on Providence, while his right one was stretched out to his – his savage children. And there was Ludjee, whom he had later renamed Lalla Rookh. What a little minx she had been, but she had aged so quickly. Ah well, them were the days. Indeed, he had fought the good fight and reaped the rewards of his noble actions; but as he gazed at the sketch, it seemed to recede into a far past when he had believed and trusted not in the things of man, but in his own spirit, and that of Providence, of course. Now he had to rely on persons such as that woman; but then, had it been any better before? Other images came. Sad, sad images of natives lying dying or dead. No fault of his though. In the dispute between the races, those who failed to evolve went down. He had soothed their pillows when it was apparent that all the government wanted was for them to be out of sight and mind. If only he had been given the resources, his experiment in civilising would have been a success, as it could be here. Well, he had resigned in the face of government intransigence and returned home where, with his modicum of fame and his government pension, plus the returns from a few investments he had made, he had managed to live comfortably, though was not well off. His old urge for adventure, and perhaps his need for a second chance, had led him to return to the colonies; and if he could make the gold and this land his, why, he could save these poor savages. Thinking thus, he decided that it was time for him to visit the native camp. He would take Monaitch with him, using him just as he had tame savages in the old days to initiate contact with their wilder brethren.

Sir George used to get his sable friends to strip before approaching uncivilised natives; but when he approached Monaitch, he received a resounding, 'No!' Monaitch was a Christian: he had been saved from his savage ways and did not wish to return to them. Clothing, no matter how ragged, was a sign of his new status.

'I not do it,' he declared. 'Jesus has entered my life and also new ways. I naked and ashamed and He taught me to be clothed and unashamed. I am one of elect now.'

Again Sir George wondered to which sect the missionary who had converted Monaitch had belonged. He certainly had not been of the Established Church. Once, Sir George himself had been of the same persuasion: he had gone out to Christianise and civilise the natives. Monaitch was an example of success, though it was not his success and this rankled. Still, relying on his old methods of conciliation, he needed a native companion to establish confidence and so he agreed to Monaitch keeping his rags.

They walked along the track which led from the water down into the gully and up the other side to meander towards the natives' camp. Sir George listened for their chatter, but there was only silence. Perhaps they were out hunting? Not even a crow squawked, and the hot sun beat down upon the desolate landscape. Only the flies buzzed about his face, settling down at the corners of his eyes to get at the moisture. He brushed them away as he walked, feeling the perspiration start from his face and body. This reminded him of Mrs Fraser and how, even covered from head to foot in a heavy cloth, she never appeared to be discomfited by the heat; though during the day she was enervated and came alive only in the evening. Well, some might be like that, but not he. The perspiration dribbled down his backbone and, by the time the strangely silent camp lay before him, his face was flushed, and worse, the heat had caused a rash on his skin that itched incessantly.

Sir George was not in a good frame of mind as he entered the camp to find the natives grouped about a central fire. He stopped aghast. Before them lay the body of a child and, my God, what were they doing but preparing it for cooking – and eating. They were cannibals!

Another man might have withdrawn, but not Sir George. 'Stop, stop,' he shrilled out. 'Stop in the name of God,' and he strode towards the accusing eyes of the natives. 'This is not right,' he accused them in return.

'They not understand you, nor understand me,' Monaitch told him. 'They from desert and have own lingo.'

'Well, does that alter things?' Sir George declared. 'Their ways are evil ways. They are cannibals, sir. They eat their children, sir. A stop must be put to it and I will do so; if not this day, soon!'

'They are pagans,' Monaitch declared in turn. 'Praise the Lord, I have been saved.' And he began singing:

'Can we, whose souls are lighted
With wisdom from on high,
Can we to men benighted
The lamp of life deny?
Salvation! oh, salvation!'

He raised his hands on high and would have flopped onto his knees, if Sir George had not grabbed him; for Sir George was thinking of a time when he had had to escape such savages with spears whistling around him. These too were hostile. He had been foolhardy to come among them with only a single companion and, what was more, a Bible-basher.

He stood there irresolutely. It was then that one of the women, old with sagging belly and breasts, picked up the dead infant and, holding it in her arms, began a high keening which set his nerves on edge. She advanced towards him with her awful burden.

'My God,' the knight exclaimed, 'she is about to offer me that dead child for my meal. It is how things were done in the south island when they speared a kangaroo and offered me a portion. This is too terrible, horrible!' And he turned and fled from the camp. The woman stopped her wailing and stared after him.

Monaitch turned and came after Sir George, who was already out of the wadi and into the police encampment. Such a great Christian, Monaitch thought. Such was his faith that the very sight of a heathen ritual caused him so much pain that he could not abide it. With this thought in his mind, when he came to Sir George, he said: 'It time for us good Christians to kneel and pray for benighted souls. We call on the Lord to reach into hearts so they forsake Devil's ways.'

'I say amen to that,' Sir George declared. 'I shall hold a general prayer meeting tonight; but now I must write up my report. Such customs should not go unrecorded. They will act as incentives for others to bring Christ into their lives. A mission must be established here as soon as possible. Cannibals, cannibals.'

'Amen, amen!' Monaitch shouted.

Sir George lifted an arm, then went into his tent to describe on paper what he had just witnessed. Before this, however, he was so upset that he needed a brandy or two to settle his nerves. It pained him to begin on his last bottle.

CHAPTER SEVEN

Amelia Fraser was a widow by day, a girl with woman's eyes in the evening, and sometimes a bat by night. All three could be considered prey and now, as a bat, she found herself hunted as a bat. Pursued, she took refuge underground which, although it heightened her powers and endurance, did not put her in the best of moods. It was not an unfamiliar place for she had passed a sojourn there before, but the natives and their cursed shaman had trapped her there, and taken her man from her. She sighed at the memory, and her anger rose to push her through the tunnel that led in the direction of her goal. At least this way she could avoid the light of day, but she vowed that if she came across the owlman again, he would suffer. It was only because she was carrying the letter and thus was impeded in her manoeuvrability that she had had to stop the conflict. Besides that, he was a huge fellow and might have inflicted harm before she was able to drain him dry.

Bat had fewer problems with the darkness and stillness than with her thoughts; but at a number of intersections with other tunnels, she felt the presence of things alien enough to be avoided. Her keen ears detected slithering movements betokening the writhing of vast things, perhaps too gigantic for her to handle. She increased her speed rather than diminished it, especially when something entered the tunnel and pushed after her.

Finally, she came to an inclined passageway and went up it to emerge into a cave with a circle of light at the far end. Damn, it was still day. At least that thing was no longer after her. Well, the night could not be long in coming and then she would continue her journey above ground, where she would have the stars to settle her mind.

The evening came none too soon for her, for she was feeling her loneliness and her need for that man who had gone off from her without a by-your-leave. Well, he was voyaging on a whaler now, but sooner or later she would see him again. She knew it from the prescience which came with her condition. With that thought, she darted from the cave and headed southwards to the town. The night was peaceful with the stars glittering above as hard as eyes.

Her mind had settled by the time she swooped around the bungalow and flew along the verandah to Lucy's room. She needed the girl's company as much as her blood, and was about to transform when duty called. The letter had to be given to the governor as soon as possible. Well, to the town to find a messenger, for the old chap would not like to have a bat, nor a naked woman, intrude upon his drinking. Reluctantly she flew down into the darkened and near-deserted town. Only a few lights and, judging by the noise and the smell, one came from a tavern. She changed into her human shape and waited in the shadows. The door opened and a man came through. He stopped near where she was hiding and there came the sound of rushing water. He was pissing. When he was shaking out the last drops, she touched his shoulder. He let go an oath and jerked around to find a naked white woman beside him. He was so startled that he left his prick hanging out.

Finally, he managed to get out: 'My God, a naked white woman!'

Amelia grabbed his head in both her hands and pulled his face close to hers. She gazed deeply into his eyes in a fixed stare that gained her mastery. He became still and did not even become aroused when she stroked him. She felt the blood coursing through his veins and her hunger rose. She roughly pushed his face, twisting it away to reveal the neck, and was about to sink her fangs into the throbbing artery when she recovered control of herself. Keeping her eyes locked with his, she stepped back and ordered: 'This letter is to be taken to the governor immediately. See to it.'

He stared at the letter in his hands and was about to stumble off, when she said 'Hold!' The man stopped and she went to him and tucked in his penis. 'Mrs Crawley might be interested in that, but not the governor,' she said with a laugh and sent him on his way. As Bat, she swooped over him to check that he was on the right track, then went ahead to the bungalow.

Now as Mela, she tapped on her friend's door and pushed it open. Lucy sat on the bed with her tapestry stretched before her. She was putting the finishing touches to the scene her friend had sketched for her. The young girl looked up and cried out when she saw who was standing there. She rushed into Mela's arms.

'Sweetest, I missed you,' Mela murmured to the young wife of that Sir George. She held her away and gazed into her fair face. Hungrily, she stared at the vein throbbing in the girl's neck while she explained that she had come from the goldfields and that her mode of travel meant that she had had to go naked and now needed to borrow some clothing.

Lucy was selfish enough to accept her Mela's arrival as but the strength of their love: a love which could move mountains, or in this case, cause her friend to come to her all naked and open.

'I need to cover myself,' Mela murmured, to which her dearest replied, 'And a bath too, for you pong.' Then happily, she bustled about, flinging open the wardrobe and hunting for a suitable costume. They were of the same physique and indeed, as had been noted before, appeared as sisters; at least, did so in the evening when Amelia could fling off her widow's weeds. Now Lucy took as much delight in dressing her friend as she once did in costuming her dolls. She threatened her Mela with stays and touched her friend's breasts to see if they were as firm as she maintained when she tossed the constricting garment aside. At last Amelia stood dressed in one of the filmy muslin frocks the girl favoured, though she was a married woman.

'Now, somewhat respectable, I am ready to see the governor's wife,' Amelia told her. 'And I must feed for I am famished.'

'Yes, but your hair. It needs to be washed and dressed properly. O, what can I do with it?' Lucy rushed to get her brushes and combs and, as she worked, complained: 'This place is like a museum with that old governor and his frump of a wife. Her London is long gone and yet she persists in talking about it. Why, that mad king must have been still alive when she was there. I hope I never grow as old as she,' the girl declared.

'And perhaps you won't either,' Amelia said with a smile, avoiding kissing her friend fully on the lips, owing to the rankness of her breath. Instead, she pressed her mouth against the girl's neck and let the hidden flow of blood tickle her lips. Since she had been away, the girl had recovered her strength; how the blood dinned in her veins.

'Enough, enough,' Amelia said, as much to herself as to her companion. 'No time, no time. There, the comb runs smoothly, the tangles are out and I must be about. Tie it behind and then get that woman to me. Hurry, you little goose, for there is a fellow coming with a letter from your husband to the governor. Of course, he has not written one for you, but that is the way of men. I have to be sure that the messenger reaches the governor this night. That woman will see to it when she knows the reason.' And she pushed away the pouting Lucy, who had returned with a wet handkerchief to clean a few smudges from Mela's face before going off on her errand.

Amelia impatiently walked up and down, stopping occasionally to stare at the tapestry which was rich with the colours of the land. Would the woman come, and quickly at that? A hard rap came at the door, and Lucy was pushed aside as Rebecca swished in, all bulky skirts as faded as her looks.

'How is it that you are here, Mrs Fraser?' she demanded. 'It is a long way to come for a social visit. The back of beyond prove too much for you? I thought you doted on naked savages and desolate spaces –'

'No time for that,' Amelia hissed. 'I have only one word to say: gold!'

'Gold!' exclaimed the woman, her eyes lighting up at the word. 'Gold.' She repeated the word greedily and her hands clenched as if about the precious metal itself.

'Yes, gold, and we must move quickly to get it for ourselves. There are hundreds of fossickers out there and they are everywhere. I have rushed back so that we can forestall them. I have seen, Mrs Crawley, with my own eyes a slug of gold too large for me to shift. We need to possess the land on which it was found. Sir George wishes to be given a grant for it. This will enable him to bar the prospectors. Moreover, to hide our intent, the land grant is to be for him to build a mission to conciliate the natives thereon. Your husband must draw up the Deed tonight. I am here secretly, and for our own benefit. Your husband must not know of my presence. There is a letter which will be delivered shortly to him with the necessary details and coordinates. It will enable him to draw up the Deed. Get him to do it this night, for I must return. It is a long and dusty trip, but worth it with the stakes so high.'

'Gold, gold, a huge nugget,' Rebecca Crawley exclaimed, all thought of Amelia's unlikely presence driven from her mind. 'At last something good comes from this wretched colony. And what is to be my share? Once, I put myself out for others and all that I got out of it was exile. I will not be duped again.'

'Work that out with Sir George when he arrives here. I am but the messenger,' Amelia replied abruptly. 'He is a hypocrite, perhaps a rogue; but the power resides with the governor.'

'That man with power!' Rebecca said derisively. 'I am the one, not him. He has sunk down into the depths of this land and is fit only to sit in his chair and lift his glass to his withered lips. It is I who make the decisions, write his reports and even guide his faltering hand in signing them. If there is gold – and why would you lie? – my share is already in my hand.'

'First settle the matter, then think of the spoils. There is no time to dither, for I hear the messenger's feet on the verandah. Settle it tonight!'

'It shall be, it shall be, for Rebecca Crawley has never been found wanting when there is a deed to be done. I was about to put in place a licence scheme to siphon off what I could from those diggers, but that is petty indeed in the face of your claim, though nonetheless it will be done. Well, I'll see to it.'

'Do the Deed and soon you shall be plunging your arms up to the elbow in gold nuggets. Or, if you wish to try your strength, seek to move that slab of gold in the shape of a fleece which might have come from the ram of Neptune himself.'

'Well, I am for it. There is only one port to the colony and I shall be on my guard.' And with this, the woman rushed from the room to do the needful.

'It is a simple enough matter to deal with greed,' Amelia observed to Lucy, as she began divesting herself of her borrowed clothing. 'And dear, don't turn your head so daintily. We have lain in each other's arms, and when I came your eyes were all over me. How sweet, the vein pulsing in your neck. It draws me, but I need you as you are; later I will sip a little from you. And, when I return, I will sketch a few more scenes for your tapestry.'

She stood there a moment, naked and with a hungry expression on her face then, filled with her need, she leapt through the door.

'I'll have to get a bath ready for you,' the girl said to the open door.

As Amelia reached the verandah, she was already changing into her chiropteran form. Into the night sky she darted, and to the road where the man, after delivering the letter, was making his way back to the town. His eyes were still glazed, though as he walked along he suddenly regained his senses and, for the world of it, could not think why he had drifted out of his way. The last thing he remembered was leaving the tavern to relieve himself. What had caused him to go along the road towards the governor's bungalow? He was shaking his head when an apparition appeared in front of him.

'My God, a naked white woman!' he exclaimed.

The woman lashed out with a shapely foot and kicked him in the groin, effectively making the words his last, though his mouth was opening and closing as if he did wish to speak on. This lasted only an instant as he was doubling up in agony, except that the naked white woman did not wish him to fall to the ground. She straightened him up with hands that were stronger than human and then ripped at his neck. The agony caused him to attempt to scream; but the lips at his neck shifted to his mouth and sucked at his tongue. It extended to be bitten off. The woman spat it out and returned to his neck. Now he began to make the last sounds he would make in this life. A hideous series of retching, gurgling noises that were loud enough to reach the tavern. The sound of clinking bottles ceased. The uncanny silence seemed to be filled with straining ears; but there was nothing much to be heard. Only a slurping which did not carry far.

The noise from the bar began again with loud calls for drinks.

Amelia finished off her meal and cast away the drained husk, upset because she had been so overcome by hunger that she had not played with her victim and had emptied him as nothing more than a container of liquid sustenance. She stared at the bloodless corpse, then picked it up and ran towards the sea. His blood had been rich and she expended in that wild run some of the energy which filled her. Now she was at the heads. On one side lay the open sea, on the other the wide bay. She flung the body from her and watched as it splashed into the ocean. It went under and came to the surface. For some reason, she sat down, staring at the corpse bobbing up and down in the ebb and flow of the waves. A deep sigh came from her and she said to herself: I wonder how that whaler man of mine fares? Well, they say that the sea after a time casts its rubbish onto the beach, and when it does I'll be there to – well, to greet him.

She sighed again, got to her feet, transformed and darted out to sea. Still in sight of land, the bat suddenly struggled to turn. It seemed that some force had attempted to control her direction. Now, she freed herself and turned back to the land.

Government House had an absence of servants, except for a woman who was supposed to fill in as a cook and do whatever else needed doing. She did the cooking and left the rest, unless reminded every few minutes. She had not taken to the slip of a girl who had managed to snare the old gentleman for a husband, and she ignored Lucy's request for buckets of hot water to fill the bath tub which had to be borrowed from Mrs Crawley and brought to her chamber. After a deal of shifting to accommodate it, the woman left disgruntled. Finally, it was Lucy herself who went to the kitchen and heated up a huge cauldron, the water from which she carried in a bucket to her room. The bucket was heavy, but she was young and in love, so by the time her friend arrived the bath tub was ready for her. There was not enough room for both of them, but Mela needed it more than Lucy did. Since her first visit, Mela had managed to get spots of sticky stuff on face; but it scrubbed off more easily than the dust of her journey, which lay thickly on her and discoloured the water to a lightish pink.

Lucy washed and caressed her friend, shifting her about as she washed this arm and the other, this leg and that, then began on her thighs. Amelia lay back in the soapy warm water, feeling replete and at ease, more than she had done for some time. She sighed as the girl's gentle fingers began playing with her pubic hair. From far away Mela heard her giggle as she said: 'You're not dry like last time.'

She awoke from her doze in alarm, to find the water cold and the girl still beside the tub. Amelia murmured and pulled herself out. Through the top of the window she saw that the sky was lightening with the dawn and that too soon the sun would be peering in. She rushed to the window and covered it over with a blanket; not content with that, she pushed a large cushion against it. With the room dark and safe for a time, she allowed her friend to come to her with a towel. Lucy dried the upper part of Mela's body, then she knelt, doing her thighs and legs. Already the day was draining Amelia of strength and she let the girl push her back on the bed.

Lucy took her chum's feet into her lap, dried them and then raised one up to suck at the toes. 'Now you'll have to stay with me,' she whispered softly. 'It's broad daylight outside and you'll be seen if you try to leave, and that old hag hasn't returned yet. Anyway, the bed is wide enough for both of us and since we've both been up all night we need to rest.'

Lucy fussed over Amelia, pushing her playfully to one side as she got the yellowed sheet over her. As she did so, there was a knock on the door and Amelia had just time to pull a blanket completely over herself before it was flung open to let in a flow of light. Mrs Crawley strode through with a letter in her hand.

'Sweet Jesus,' she exclaimed. 'It has taken me the whole night long to get the Deed written and signed. Where is she? Asleep, I bet, while I do the work. God, that husband of mine. I know what is best, but he persists in trying to think. Of course, no one trusts Sir George. Sorry, dear, but – well, he's your bread and butter and it's best not to have too high an opinion of him. Look to your best interests. If a wife does what is expected of her, she can get her husband to do her bidding, or other men for that matter. Anyway enough of that, there is the Deed. Let her rest, for she has a long trip ahead of her to get it to where it must go. Sweet Lord, these modern women and their urge to outdo the men. Well, let them. I have my ways of getting beyond them which bring in even bigger dividends.'

'The journey tired her out. Poor dear, she's completely exhausted,' Lucy replied.

'So am I, but I'm not in my bed,' Mrs Crawley retorted, eyeing the covered figure. 'Such a strange bold woman, she is. She reminds me of that woman I met in Germany, what was her name? It will come to me. She was quite ugly, repellent, more like a man than a woman. Ah, yes, Grafin Ida Hahn-Hahn, a traveller of some renown. She published an account of her adventures in German and so I was spared reading it. Your little friend is much like her; but instead of an ugliness, she has a beauty which is just as repellent. But what is this to me as long as our acquaintanceship is profitable? Give her the letter. She need not see me until the matter is settled.' And with this, she marched out of the room, leaving the door wide open. The full light of day streamed in.

Lucy rushed to close it then went to Amelia and uncovered her head, then, on impulse, the rest of her. She caressed her languid chum as she exclaimed: 'Such a virago, but it should be the last of her we see this day. They are not ones for breakfast either and so I need not put in an appearance. Now, let me get into bed with you. I need to rest too and right against you.'

She undressed, taking off first her skirt and bodice, then her underskirt and crinoline hoop, then her stays, which were of the new fashion and fastened up in front, and last of all, her pantalets. She stretched, uncrimping her body from the clothing that had confined and contained it, then naked slipped into bed and snuggled up close to her sweetheart. She rested her cheek against her friend's breasts and began gently to snore.

A somnolent Amelia gazed down upon her. 'Silly goose,' she whispered. 'There are not many who would sleep so tenderly in my arms without a qualm.'

It was dark when Lucy floated out of a delicious swoon. She lay there in the tender afterglow, her bruised neck aching only slightly, feeling, instead of weak, ravenously hungry. She caressed the imprint left by the body beside her and lay there smiling awhile, before getting up and dressing for dinner. As she did so, she mused over how fate had brought her Mela. Fancy, she had had to come to the ends of the earth to find a friend to replace Mina, who had drifted away from her after Lucy had married. At least her new friend was not so stodgy. She was an adventuress who could cross over trackless miles of desert for a tryst. Such a sweet, sweet, kind friend. She smiled, eyeing the next scene Mela had sketched for her to embroider: a lake with native people camped close by, and Sir George addressing them. But her Mela was not drawn in, and Lucy sighed.

Amelia had sipped on Lucy's blood as one would sample a rare wine. She too went over the tender encounter as she bent her bat's wings and thrust on through the night. Again impeded by a letter, it would not be possible for her to complete the long journey that night. She would take shelter in that cave, but had no intention of going down those ghastly underground tunnels, even if they would shorten her trip. No, she would go above ground, owlman or no owlman.

The first night passed uneventfully, as did the following day. By the time evening arrived so had the pangs of hunger. She needed to slake her thirst and, as she flew on, she kept her eyes open for prey. If she could not find a human, an animal would do. She kept putting off her feeding and was ravenous by the time she spied the dull campfires of a native encampment. Down she swooped. There was no one awake to notice the wheeling form of the bat as it sped between the huts. Suddenly, it lurched and sank onto the ground.

Amelia had sensed the presence of Owl shaman. She could smell him and even enter into the stream of his turgid thoughts, which told her that he was in his human form and asleep. She drifted a little along his thought stream, but when the currents shifted and whirlpools began to form she withdrew, fearing that he was sensing her psychic presence within his mind. These native doctors had strong powers and she had no wish to disturb him and raise the monster. Feeding was uppermost in her thoughts, not a fight. She set about finding her drinking vessel.

She changed into her human form and, holding the letter in one hand, went and peered into a hut. A woman lay there and beside her were two children. Amelia chose the boy, picked him up easily and made off with him. Safely away from the camp and that owlman, she sat on the ground, put down the letter beside her, rocked the infant for a moment, then pressed a hand over his mouth as she bent and pierced his neck. The blood was fresh and young. It flowed without any excessive sucking and the infant's weak struggles soon stopped. She sucked the last drops of blood from his empty veins, then stood with the tiny body in her arms. How might she dispose of it? She walked to where the ashes of one of the fires still glowed and placed the body on it, then she flung some boughs on top so that it might blaze up and alarm the natives. She ran back to her letter, transformed and took it up, then darted into the sky.

'Well, as I've had the blood they can have the flesh,' she thought as she flashed towards the oasis.

CHAPTER EIGHT

Sir George liked to linger over a snifter or two of brandy in the evening. Of course, in this desolation there had been no sense in packing a goblet and so he had to make do with a mug. He filled this ungainly vessel and slowly savoured the first mouthful. He had always liked a good drop, though too often had had to make do with a bad one; but since his fame, his civil-list pension, plus his speculations, he had the means to gratify his taste for fine wines and liquors. This evening, because of his uneasiness, he quickly finished the brandy and poured himself another, though it was his last bottle. Darkness had fallen on the land with no twilight to speak of, nor had the heat lessened. It was too enervating for him to take notes for his report, although he had tried conscientiously. This meant only that he had stared at the blank sheet of paper in front of him. With his second mug of brandy before him, he did pick up the pen, but his fingers were slippery with sweat. He watched a drop of moisture fall to stain the paper, then put down his pen and thought about the letter he had dispatched to the governor. Had the woman sent it on its way? She seemed to have gone along with it, leaving him to fling a scrap or two at the dingo which mournfully hung about her empty tent. How long before the letter reached the town, and how quickly the governor? The fellow wasn't much chop, but his wife seemed to be the one with brains and thus one to cultivate as an ally. She was certainly dissatisfied and this could be turned to his advantage. Not the governor though. An old military man from a good family, he had fallen into the lassitude common to those with political connections who find themselves in charge of virtually nothing at the far borders of the empire. Well, the way to a husband was often through the wife and Mrs Crawley might come through in his favour. But what would be her price? That was the question.

Unable to speculate further, Sir George poured himself another drink, sadly emptying the bottle. Now it would have to be rum, just like in the old days. A rum do, he thought, slightly slurring the words even in his mind as it reached out to his last mission on the south island which had proved a field of profitable endeavour.

'I was like a father to them,' he said aloud. 'Well, almost,' he amended, for into his mind slipped a naked native woman, all brown breasts and fluid hips, who had served him well and truly. His member stirred as he thought of her. A native queen and so he had named her Lalla Rookh. He grunted as he remembered her mouth on him and that subtle trick she had. It was then that the image of Mrs Fraser came to put all lasciviousness to rest. So stern and severe, looking like a girl but with the hard eyes of an experienced woman. It was those eyes that repelled as much as attracted him; but could he put his trust in such a one?

How hot and dry it was, though his body oozed moisture. The brandy had made the perspiration flow from him like a veritable torrent. He poured himself a drink of tepid water, flung it down and, feeling stifled in the tent, pulled the flap aside and went out into the open where it was scarcely any better. At the police lines the black constables were having their evening meal. Mrs Fraser's tent was still and unillumined. The dingo stirred and raised its head to regard him sadly. Where had that woman got to and what about his letter? Had he warned her of the natives and their treachery? Well, he must wait until she deigned to appear. Across the slight declivity in which the pool rested was the tent of the two prospectors, one of whom was his son. He would go and have a word with him, taking the opportunity to assert his parental authority again.

As he approached, he saw two figures: the slight one must be Sonny and, of course, the large one was that Russian. He slowed as he neared to see what they were up to. It was not Sonny, but – and his ire rose – a young native girl of about sixteen and, as with these people, in the prime of her womanhood. How quickly these females aged and it was best to get them as soon as they blossomed. Such firm and well-shaped breasts, the hips rounded, the legs were on the thin side, but the face was pleasing and she looked quite clean, as if she had recently plunged into the pool. Still, it was not right that a white man, even a Russian, could dine on equal terms with a native. It was one thing that he had never done.

He strode into the firelight and stood there glowering. The Russian ignored him and continued eating.

'This, sir, will not do,' Sir George stated, noticing that his voice, because of the dust and dryness, had become harsh. He liked the effect and continued on firmly. 'Don't encourage these people. Before you know it they'll be hanging about the camp, begging and thieving.'

'Russian Jack's always ready to share his meal, and this is but a slip of a girl. A kitten of a girl.' The man grinned at his companion.

'Females are their spies, sir. They send them in and the next thing is that you'll have the men down on you. The jealousy. These are savages –'

'Savages or not, they're still human beings. They done me no wrong and I'll do them no wrong.'

'Take care, sir, take care. They speared that teamster and you'll be the next. I can't allow it, I can't allow it. She must go, must go,' he grated. 'The safety of the camp is at risk.'

'This is my camp and Russian Jack'll share with those he wants to. None of your business. Keep to your own side of the pool if you don't like it.'

'What, what?' spluttered Sir George. 'Just you wait.' When this land is mine, then you'll be the one to go, he thought.

'But, you know,' the giant said with a huge grin, 'those I do welcome and have a yarn with – well, my flask is empty and the price to share my fire is some of that rum you lot have got stashed away.'

Sir George made no reply. He watched as the girl finished shovelling the beans and pork into her mouth with her hand, then licked the plate. She took up a pannikin and had a long drink. Her eyes gleamed over the rim and he thought he saw an inviting look there. The little minx, he thought, staring as she poured the rest of the water over her hand, got to her feet and stretched, displaying her naked charms for him. His eyes travelled over her. The pert breasts, the broad hips and the vee of her groin. An almost perfect example of native womanhood, he thought. One which Mrs Fraser might sketch with the flair she had to render the figures of women. The girl stood there a moment, full on to him so that he could see the scanty hair decorating rather than hiding her slit. He rose to the occasion and to his fullest extent as she turned, her buttocks undulating as she swayed past him. Unable to help himself, he watched her leave the light.

'That's a sight to stir the Devil,' the Russian said, with a comical leer.

Hoarsely, Sir George replied: 'I must get clothes on them. It is shameful.'

'But a sight for sore eyes,' Russian Jack commented. 'But about that little matter of the rum ...?'

'A child of nature,' Sir George murmured, his mind still on the female.

'Well, with a bit of luck, you can get her. Hear tell they couple the young ones with the old men and they don't get enough. Then the old blighters, they're willing to lend them out, for a piece of pork or a quid of baccy.'

'Sir, sir, they are not to be taken advantage of like that. They're savages, savages,' Sir George replied, recovering not only his prudishness but his snobbishness. Russians were, after all, close to savages themselves. Why, they still had serfs and, what was it called? *Droit du seigneur.*

'I'll see about that rum,' he said, moving away, hoping that his excitement wouldn't be revealed to the man's sardonic gaze.

But as he went back towards his tent, he was still aroused. His mind drifted back to the time when he had had one of them. He had been superintendent of that mission and was having his tot of rum when the native woman came in. He had known her when she had been young and though she was getting on in years, there was still something about her. Ludjee, ah yes, the one and only Lalla Rookh. In she came, and by then he had had them all decorously dressed in loose shifts so that there was not that constant temptation before him. He had been examining a set of curious playing cards that he had obtained from a seaman, which were of anthropological or social interest. They were decorated with couples engaging in various obscenities. He had been flipping them over when she had entered and as an experiment he had shown them to the woman.

She had merely glanced over them with dull eyes and said: 'Ghost lady and man together.'

'Look closer,' he had urged her.

The cards were lying scattered on his desk and she had lowered her head to see them. He got to his feet and went behind her. She continued looking, bent slightly over. It was easy to press her further down with one hand whilst he flung up her skirt with the other. Of course, she was bare beneath the shift and it was a mere moment to free himself and plunge inside her. It was over in a matter of seconds, but had been exquisite, one of the best he had ever had.

He remembered that he had found a similar pack of cards when in Paris and still had them. He went into his tent and to his kit. There they were. He sat at his folding table, flipping from card to card. What with the native girl and now these, he could not help but fondle himself, but soon desisted. He put the cards back, then found a bottle of rum and had a long drink. Well, he would take the rest back to the Russian, keep on his good side until the time came to order him off the land. But where was that woman? How long would he have to wait until she told him that the letter had gone?

'Here's yer rum,' he said heartily, passing the Russian the bottle and leaving before he was forced to have a drink. In truth, he was feeling somewhat woozy, and worse, his erection had returned. Hidden by the darkness, he undid his front as he went to the lip of the gully where the path went down. A figure squatted there. The girl? Mounting excitement made his hand clutch tighter. Yes! She came to her feet as he was almost on top of her, became aware of him, recoiled in fright and turned to flee.

'Too late for you, my little minx,' he muttered, grabbing her from behind and dumping her on her hands and knees, going down with her so that he was in position for the thrust. The wild thing began struggling. He had to quieten her. If she screamed ... He shifted his grip from her hips to her neck. The scream was ready to burst forth and he had to tighten his grip so that not even a whimper emerged. He thrust against her, enjoying her body, but with his hands occupied he could not guide himself where he wished to go. It did not matter, and though he spent himself without achieving his aim, it was enough. It was then that he noticed that the girl was limp as a rag under his hands. He eased his grip and she fell away and onto the ground. Leaving her there, he stumbled off and hastily fixed himself up as he hurried to his tent. He needed a drink, and of a better quality than that rum he had given the lout.

At the scene of his encounter, what appeared to be a patch of darkness flopped down beside the quiescent form. It resolved into the lighter shape of a naked white woman.

Amelia knelt and bent her face close to the girl's mouth. A faint brush of air revealed that she still lived. Yes, Amelia could feel the blood moving through her veins. The temptation was too much. Her gaping fanged mouth came down and there was a slurping sound as she began to feed. The iron smell of blood permeated the hot air. At last, she lifted her head and knelt back, then sprang up, her hand at the same instant clutching for the letter she had discarded beside her. She glided away to the waterhole where she scrubbed away any traces of her meal. Afterwards, she crept past Sir George's tent. A lantern glowed from within, casting his shadow onto the canvas. Without creating a light, and with her pet fawning about her, she selected a white frock knowing that it was reddened from the dust, pulled it over her head, buttoned it up, then ran a brush through her hair before going to the knight's tent.

'Sir George, Sir George,' she called. 'Good news. Good news, the Deed is already here from the governor. The messenger must have killed half a dozen horses under him to get there and back so quickly.'

'Wait, wait,' came the unsteady answer. After a few minutes, Sir George came out carrying the lantern. 'Yes, yes,' he exclaimed, not going on to enquire as to the swiftness of the reply, for his recent encounter had unsettled him.

Amelia, who had not prepared an answer, was relieved to see how the light was shaking in his hand. She vowed that he would remain distraught for some time. He did not realise that the girl was well and truly dead with her throat ripped out. Would he believe that he had done that when in a state of rut? She doubted it and needed to cover her tracks.

'Sir George,' she said, handing him the letter, 'this is the Deed; but something awful has happened. After I met the messenger, I came across a dead native girl on the path. Who could have done such a thing? Terrible, terrible, for her people will try to exact a bloody vengeance.'

'That miner, that miner, that Tartar.' Sir George blustered the first thing that came into his mind. 'I saw him with a native girl and warned him.' Then, confused and distressed, he changed his mind: 'Not him, not him,' he cried. 'It was the savages. They saw her with him and such is their jealousy that they have murdered her. Now they will be after us. Sergeant Barron must get his men ready to repel an attack.'

'But the native camp is quiet. Would it be so, if they had done such a thing? Perhaps someone else has done the deed,' Amelia replied, smirking as her face was in darkness. Now, what would he do about that?

'It was them,' he declared. 'It was. All our native boys are well under Barron's control. That Russian would not, nor would my son. The camp is quiet because they are sharpening their spears. I know them!'

'Still, is it not strange that she was left lying there, and that – as the stars gave some light – it appeared she had been violated?' Amelia said, licking her red lips as she relived the scene. She felt so full and bloated that she could even look at the knight's fat and sweaty neck without thinking of the thick veins pulsating beneath the skin.

'Violated, violated – that word cannot be used in regard to these savages!' Sir George almost screamed out, the hoarseness of his voice preventing him from shrilling in his usual fashion. 'They go about completely naked, open to any man's lust and welcoming it too. Perhaps, that miner ... No, it is *their* doing. We must see to our defence.'

By this time Sir George had all but convinced himself that the girl had been killed by a savage in a fit of jealousy. Yes, that was what had occurred. No doubt about it!

'So sad, so sad,' he exclaimed sincerely. 'But is it to be wondered at? They treat their women like chattels and take their lives at will. How I desire,' he cried, rising to the occasion emotionally, 'to establish a mission here to Christianise and civilise these poor creatures. It shall happen, and it will happen! This shall be in my report, though the subject would not be fit for a sketch, nor would I expect you to put yourself through viewing the body again. Poor, poor girl,' he cried.

'Poor creature indeed to have had your hands at her throat and your thing thudding against her,' Amelia replied in a low voice to keep him unsettled.

Sir George heard, but did not hear. 'What was that you said? Yes, yes, poor creature. I know your heart goes out to them too, and with this Deed we can prevent such things from happening.'

'Yes, but that is the future. I, as a woman, feel that I cannot leave one of my sex lying there like a discarded doll after a vicious child has played with her. Her body must be seen to and even made decent. Perhaps, in one of my old dresses –'

'Yes, yes, but I don't want her in the camp,' Sir George replied firmly. 'If she is left there, the savages will take her away.'

'Sir George,' Amelia said, just as firmly, 'her remains must be treated with respect. She is beyond life, but not desecration. Who knows what might happen to her poor, defiled corpse?'

'Well, if we are to do something it must be done quietly. Sergeant Barron will handle the matter. He has been on the battlefield and such sights are familiar to him. I, though, I myself, could not bring myself to view the corpse. It is unseemly.'

'But it is not exactly a crime?'

'No, they have not been taken under the protection of British law as yet.'

'I understand, you having a young wife, it would be most distressful.'

'It would be; it would be. Yes, yes, I cannot think. I am most distraught. I would see my young wife lying there, dead in the full bloom of womanhood. I cannot bring myself to see it. Such sadness and evil is abroad in this land. Such temptation. Such things, I swear to put a stop to. Yes, now that I have the means.'

'I hope so, Sir George, I sincerely do and I am ready to aid you in your philanthropy. You did such good work in the island to the south; but enough. I shall see to the sad remains with Sergeant Barron.' And so saying, Amelia, smirking, went into the darkness while an agitated Sir George retreated with the lantern into his tent where he immediately opened the letter with trembling hands. He quickly scanned the contents and almost whooped in delight. The land was his! He re-read the little note on lavender paper that accompanied the official Deed:

> Sir George, I remember how you rent the boredom of this isolated outpost, which I refuse to dignify with the title of town, with your presence and how, when you descended into the wilderness, you left your treasure behind in my safe keeping. She is well, but pensive at the absence of that which fulfils her life. She has taken to stitchery and is working a scene in which your figure is most prominent. How she misses you. I recall to her that you are on a mission of humanity and philanthropy and that we women must guard the domestic hearth while our men act on the world. It seems that in your case, actions are as swift as are your decisions. A Christian mission in the hinterland where those without the saving blood of Christ are to be brought within His fold.

Such a shepherd you are, but this note must end, for it is to be sent this night. Adieu until next we meet for our mutual benefit.

Rebecca Crawley

P.S. O, that others could be as forthright and strongwilled as you.

Sir George smiled again then turned his attention to the Deed of Grant: twenty thousand acres centred on the oasis.

Revived by the news and beside himself with joy, he decided that he could help in doing something about the girl's body. The natives were cruel and vicious and quick to punish. Worse, had they witnessed the deed? No. They had found her lying there, stained by her crime, and they had murdered her for it.

Satisfied with this conclusion, Sir George left his tent to go to the police lines to see if Amelia was consulting with Sergeant Barron about the disposal. As he walked carefully through the darkness, he saw that it could be to his advantage if the natives were to attack and were then repulsed. Such an incident would provide an incentive for establishing a hold on the area before the mission was founded. After all, in such ways had the empire expanded to its vast dimensions. Also, the news of an attack would spread and keep the fossickers away. Better yet, such an action would necessitate a police detachment to be posted to keep the country pacified. It had been a good evening's work after all.

While Sir George was on his way to Sergeant Barron, Amelia went back to the body and stared down at it. The throat was laid bare to the windpipe and even the vein had been severed. The flight back to the camp had famished her and she had not been in the mood for any niceties. The wounds were of such ferocity that no one would dispute that it had been the work of savages, unless it was put down to an unknown species of carnivorous animal. She felt tempted to leave the corpse sprawled there, to see what the policeman might surmise; but then, why not stir things up? Especially as there was that prospector who was in their way and must be gotten rid of sooner rather than later if Sir George (and of course herself) were to have the gold. He was such a giant of a man: she wanted him, too, and she would have him.

But first the girl. She lifted up the corpse and carried it down the track into the gully and up and out and towards the native camp. All was quiet.

There were about twenty wurlies, made from boughs, bark and leaves in beehive shapes, placed about a bare patch of earth which was now in relative darkness. In front of the huts, at the low doors, fires gleamed. As she watched, a fire was lit on the dark patch of earth and men gathered about it. She made this her target and glided forward, a pale white shape shining ghost-like under the starlight. Close enough, she lifted the body high over her head and flung it at the fire, emitting at the same time a cackle of devilish laughter. Sparks flew. She did not wait for a reaction but flittered away to the tent of the prospector. The exertion had made her thirsty and there was that large vessel of liquid waiting for her.

She took off her frock so that it would not be stained, then listened to the heavy breathing of the man inside. Was he alone? Yes, for she had seen that other one hanging about the police lines. How the blood rumbled through his veins. Aroused, she bent, thrusting herself under the canvas. The man was sprawling on his back. He had taken off all but his shirt and thus was exposed to her. She began to manipulate him as he came awake. His eyes jerked open and she glared into them, paralysing him, then squirmed down and nipped playfully at him with her fangs. He was indeed a giant of a man. She opened her mouth wide and then bit down. The deadly agony made him writhe in spite of her mesmerising. She reached up a hand and clamped it tightly over his mouth, spat out his penis and began to feed. Elated and secure in her strength, she let his body attempt to throw her off. She felt the screams that attempted to push past her hand. She pressed down harder, gulping down the torrent of blood quickly and so completely that few drops escaped her avid thirst.

All too soon it was over, and she had gorged herself so much that she vomited up all over him. She lay there, feeling the last tremblings as his spirit detached itself. As the final shudder began, she thrust her mouth hard against him, sucking up the remaining drops of fluid and, hopefully, his spirit. Before abandoning the corpse, her last act was to take up his penis and stuff it into his mouth.

Outside she quickly dressed, licked around her lips and chin to remove any telltale traces, then flung back her head and began to shriek. She stopped, heard the sound of rushing boots and began to scream again. As Sonny, Sergeant Barron and Sir George charged up, she gave one last screech and slid to the ground in a swoon. To add to the confusion, there began from the native camp the sounds of wailing. Amelia lay there like one dead, then she came to with a groan as Sonny went into the tent. He gave a harsh shout of horror which rose to mingle with the native wailing. Not to be outdone, the female creature sat up, gave a hideous shriek and fell back again.

CHAPTER NINE

Sergeant Barron, as an old infantry man, preferred the heavy musket, Brown Bessy, to the light cavalry carbine with which his constables had been equipped. The latter, although it had been designed to be fired from horseback, was difficult to load owing to the shortness of the barrel. But once, as with all things military, the knack had been attained, it was useful in that it could be loaded in a reclining position (and thus out of the field of fire) rather than standing upright, as was necessary with the old gun. This meant that the musket was good for straightforward formations, but not the guerrilla warfare he had seen waged so viciously against the French on the Spanish peninsula. The carbine was thus more practicable when going against savages, for if you stood upright to ram a cartridge and ball home, the chances were that there would be a spear sticking out of you by the time you had raised the ramrod.

Owing to his unfamiliarity with the weapon, Barron had had to train himself as well as his men in its loading and use. Now they all were proficient in tamping down the ball quickly and he had no doubt that his dozen men would give a good account of themselves if the natives attempted to rush the camp. Nonetheless, he had learnt a few sneaky things in his time and one of these he now employed: a keg of gunpowder over which he had heaped pebbles and stone fragments and laid a trail back to the perimeter of the camp which they would defend. With no wind to speak of and absolutely no rain, the line of black powder would remain still and dry, and ignite at the touch of a flame. Barron had seen such a weapon deployed with devastating effects, but he was still restless. He kept his men ready, but the night passed without incident. When morning arrived with its usual abruptness, he left two sentries on guard while the others had breakfast.

The sentries yawned as they eyed the short expanse before them which ended at the wadi. They knew that if the desert blackfellows attacked, it would be from the gully, which was as deep as a man was tall, with steep banks hiding the bottom from where they stood. They stared towards the heap of rocks where their 'Tarjent' had planted the magical device which he had assured them would go 'boom-boom' when necessary. All was still: there was not a sound from the camp of the wild blackfellows.

One of the sentries, warily circling the magic boom-boom, went to the lip of the gully to relieve himself. He stamped along, enjoying the way his heavy boots hit the ground. At the top of the gully, he hesitated; but he had no fear of those scrawny desert fellows, much less robust than his own people. He merely sniffed the air to catch the odour of their unwashed bodies, before fumbling at the front of his trousers. He stood right on the edge of the bank and began pissing. His urine described a yellow arc and hissed down onto the dry bed which was smooth and bare except for a few small boulders. He finished and fumbled again at his front. It was one thing to get used to wearing the nether garment, but another thing getting used to pulling out his penis when he wanted to piss and pushing it back after. The act held his attention and he did not notice an upsurge of sand in the gully bottom. Suddenly, a lithe black figure sprang out of the very earth and cast a spear which pierced the constable through the throat. He emitted a long gurgling shout which edged into a scream, before collapsing. Other blackfellows emerged and were running towards the side of the gully when the second sentry shouted and fired his weapon.

The veteran Barron quickly took control. 'Right you lot, hop to it!' he yelled at his men, then grabbed a brand from the fire and ran to the threatened section. His men rushed after him, followed by the two civilians.

'Here come the blighters!' Barron shouted, as about twenty- odd natives, covered all over with grey dust, came surging over the lip of the wadi.

'God damn, God damn!' he chanted, then added, 'Try this!' He flung the blazing brand down onto the end of the gunpowder trail.

The flame sizzled towards the natives and they made a tactical error and bunched. The line of fire hissing towards them was like a flame snake and they turned to flee. The serpent dashed into the heap of rocks. A clash of thunder sounded and with it came a rain of pebbles and stone fragments that decimated the whole mob. A cloud of dust rose. When it subsided, the lip of the gully was scattered with dead and dying savages.

Elated by his success, Barron screamed: 'Now after them, and teach the blighters a lesson! Go, get the rest of them.' His men raced away, hesitating at the scene of carnage to put out of their misery any that still lived. Sonny ran after them with a cocked pistol. The memory of the stealing of the schooner still rankled and he had a score to settle. He was the first down into the gully, and out of it; but prudently waited for the black constables to reach him before going on.

They stopped before the bunch of wurlies; such was the discipline that their 'Tarjent' had drilled into them, that they formed a line and fired a volley into the huts. Sonny, with his fancy revolving pistol, flung a shot at a bark wall. The constables, happy to be at last using their weapons against living human targets, loaded and fired a second then a third volley. The balls flashed through the bark walls and screams began, which urged them on. They charged into the camp with their weapons reversed. Colonial life was boring and, to fill in his time, Sergeant Barron had taught his men every dirty trick he had seen practised in Spain.

Now they put them to use. Heavy metal-shod butts smashed down onto any heads within striking distance. To find more victims, they used their heavy boots to kick down the flimsy walls of the huts. Sonny had fired only a single shot and without result. With the blood lust on him he sought someone to kill in revenge for the death of his mate. A black naked figure broke from a hut and raced towards him. He levelled his pistol and brought it down with one shot; but not content with this rushed in to deliver a mighty kick to the head. He followed it with another, before he saw that it was an old woman. He kicked her in her flabby breasts then looked for someone else to vent his rage on. A younger woman this time: she went down with a ball to the head. He might have hesitated if it had been a child, but it had not been. The constables were taking care of them. In an orgy of killing, they clubbed any who moved, and those with knifes hacked and slashed. Babies and infants were picked up and their heads slammed together. At last, there was not even a groan from the killing field.

'Give it to them, men! Don't let a blighter escape!' an excited Barron yelled, running up to find that the battle was over and not a living human being of the tribe remained.

'Good work, boys,' he shouted, firing his carbine into the air to bring his police constables to him.

Sonny reloaded his pistol, hoping that his father had seen him in the thick of the action. He kicked at the body of a woman, hitting her in the stomach so that air wheezed from the corpse. 'That's for me dead mate,' he muttered. 'That's for him and this one's for meself. That's the only thing I would ever touch you with, a boot.'

The constables collected about their leader and Sergeant Barron stared at their bloody carbine butts. 'You boys, you know them carbines don't grow on trees. All government property, and if one of you blackfellows have splintered a stock, I'll have your guts for garters. Anyway, you put 'em to good work.'

It was then that Sir George hurried up. He stopped to catch his breath as his eyes darted about the scene. 'Sir, sir,' he exclaimed, 'among those bodies – why, there are women and children. Sir, your men have perpetrated a massacre. Guns should not have been placed in their hands.

They have reverted to savagery, sir!'

'They have not, sir,' Barron exclaimed in turn. 'Fortunes of war, sir, fortunes of war. Women, aye, I have seen what they can do to men. That poor prospector. Did he deserve to go the way he did? A Russian, yes, but a white man for all that. Blighters attacked us and they all got what they deserved. It is what I have trained my boys for.'

'My mate, my mate,' Sonny quavered. 'He done them no wrong and they-they – you know what they did. Lucky none of them are alive, or we might do the same to them.'

'Sonny, Sonny, could you not turn the other cheek?'

'Other cheek indeed,' Barron stated in contempt. 'We're police, sir. My boys had to be blooded and this has done it. All of them came through, not one turned tail and ran like a mangy dog.'

'O God, O God,' Sir George moaned, thinking of what this might do to his reputation as a conciliator of savages. 'My mission, my mission! If this should get out, I'm ruined, ruined. I am here to help these poor benighted creatures and now I bear witness to a massacre. Lord, Lord, how shall I report it?'

'Don't worry, guv'nor,' Barron replied with a smirk. 'Don't worry, you yourself are a witness to their attack. And now you are witness to frontier justice. A short, quick, bloody battle in which we administer a sharp lesson to the blighters. They won't dare come near us again. And if you're squeamish about the bodies – well, simple enough matter to lay them to rest. My boys'll toss them into those huts and set them afire.'

'You will? It will be for the better, definitely for the better. But those huts are flimsy, Sergeant,' Sir George declared, his panic subsiding.

'No problem, sir, no problem at all. We'll heap the bodies up, then pile the material of the huts on them. That'll do it and the whole lot'll go up like tinder. The bark and branches are good and dry. Soon you won't even know that a battle occurred here.'

'And those corpses in front of the camp?'

'The ones that you will mention in your report, sir? The attacking warriors? Nasty skirmish, but we came through without a casualty. I'll get that cleaned up too. In this heat, if we don't, the blighters will stink to high heaven in an hour or three. Well, my boys have been sitting around on their black arses and the work'll give them something to do. Settle them down too. Now, I'll get just get myself a souvenir ...'

He marched to a male body and took out his clasp knife. He cut off its scrotum, pressed out the testes and looking into Sir George's horrified eyes, said: 'It makes a good tobacco pouch when dried. Want one for yourself? These should be in better condition than the ones at the gully.

Good talking point back in the old country, it'll make. Might even get a couple of quid for it; but you don't have to care about that.'

Sir George stared down at the scrotum with what he believed was scientific interest. He had already noticed that the native men slit their phalluses; they too were of interest. Perhaps he might pickle one.

'Ethnopornography,' he muttered to himself, then said: 'Such keepsakes are not to my liking; but then again such mementoes are symbols of this savage land and worth scientific study. They are not Christians and so their bodies are unholy and can become objects of research in this case. Well, well, I shall accept one when it has dried sufficiently, though it is such a barbaric native custom that I am loathe to.'

'More likely a Spanish custom,' Barron said dryly. 'It was what they did to the Frenchies on the peninsula. Put the fear of God back into them Frogs, you know. Worst thing you could do to a man, and I've heard they did it when many of them were alive. I could tell you a thing or two about that campaign –'

'No, no, Sergeant, I do not wish to hear more. What I do wish to have done, and speedily, is the disposal of these bodies. Most distressing, most distressing.'

'Right, Sir George. Glad to see that you're not like some of those mealy-mouthed ones they usually send out to the colonies.' Barron turned to his men and shouted to them to pile up the bodies. 'Get to it, or they'll be stinking to high heaven before you know it,' he yelled.

'Why their balls when the other is of more interest with that subincision?' a female voice enquired in Sir George's ear.

'Madam, you should not be here on this scene of carnage,' the knight spluttered. 'It is too horrific for the female sensibility. It will affect you adversely.'

'Sir George, I was a prisoner of these natives and my eyes have suffered the sight of their obscene customs. It has hardened me to such scenes.' Mrs Fraser's voice held a delighted shudder which caused Sir George to stare at her for a long instant. Seeing nothing but the black veil and a shadow from the wide peak of the bonnet, eventually he glanced away, and placed himself in front of her, to shield her from the unseemly sight, even though this brought him in closer proximity to her.

Sir George had found the woman somewhat repellent during the days she had sat at his side in the bughi, and this impression had deepened. Her increasing callousness he found repugnant, especially in one of the weaker sex, though he sought to excuse it as being the result of her experiences at the hands of the savages. In spite of this, her magnetic aura did repulse him, and any pleasantries he attempted failed to break through her icy reserve. He felt this now as she stood there completely covered from head to toe in her widow weeds with not one patch of skin revealed. As he regarded. the woman, he could not help thinking that she appeared as an apparition from some dense Gothic novel such as he had forbidden his own gentle wife to read. He noticed that the black constables, as they went about their ghastly business, darted glances at her. They must think that she was some sort of devil or demon emerged from the recesses of their no doubt hideous mythologies. He was certain that they would never regard her as a mother, as those savages had his first wife on the south island. Sir George saddened at the thought of his first wife, then brightened up as he recalled her funeral. She had been coarse and callow and a suffering unto him. That was God's truth and he was well rid of her.

'So awful,' the woman now declaimed, finally revealing that there did indeed beat a female heart under her clothing. 'Such an awful tragedy. I did not realise it. Women and children foully murdered. Infants with their tiny skulls bashed in. What other indignities have been inflicted on them as their poor naked bodies lay open and defenceless against the soiling touches of those brutal black police constables? Sir George, report this evil deed. These natives are but children of nature and did not deserve to be put down like animals. And why is a fire being kindled above them? As animals they were slaughtered and now are we to see them eaten as animals?'

'God forbid, madam; God forbid. This is terrible, terrible – women and children massacred; but, but, they would have done the same to us. It was the survival of the fittest.'

The bark and branches caught with a whoosh. The flames shot up into the limpid sky along with the reek of scorching flesh.

'There is a piquancy about burning flesh which almost makes one wish to try it,' Amelia observed in a tone which confused Sir George. How could she become so light-hearted about such a thing, when a moment ago she had been bewailing the massacre of women and children? Well, at least with this attitude she would not be spreading tales about him.

'And are you sure that these savage constables won't begin a ghastly feast in front of me? Could I bear such a sight?'

There was more than a hint of sarcasm in her voice; but the very idea upset Sir George and he took her words at face value. 'Sergeant Barron,' he called. 'Sergeant Barron, are your men under control? Might not their savage natures assert themselves under the influence of the aroma of cooking flesh?'

'These ain't your cannibal savages at all,' Barron declared in amusement. 'Never caught them at it yet and never will. They have a horror of it.'

'Well, that may be true,' the knight replied to set his mind at ease. 'But this day, they have fought a battle. They are overexcited.'

'Along with your son, who was in the thick of things when I came on the scene; but as I've said, this is frontier justice, quick and, once done, over with. They're as calm as you or me now. Now, please excuse me, I've got to see about them bodies in front of the camp. I'll collect them in the wadi and then think how to get rid of them.'

'Yes, yes, it is the best thing to do. This, this frontier justice is hard to accept. I am but newly arrived in the colony, and to see such a thing when I am on a commission of mercy to the very ones that have been slaughtered ... I fear, sir, that the news will get out.'

'Sir George,' Amelia observed, 'my female heart went out to the poor creatures. I suffered agonies at first, then that poor mutilated prospector seemed to appear before my eyes and he smiled. Laugh, if you will, at my female sensitivity; but such are we. Your male mind can review what these savages have done without pity or cause, unlike we poor women who find it hard to accept that what has been done was necessary to have been done. I have seen enough here for a thousand days of nightmares.' And with that, she turned and retreated from the burning pyre.

Sir George mentioned the little matter of wanting a native phallus for scientific purposes and Sergeant Barron said that he would see if he could find an undamaged specimen, then they followed after the woman to see to the other bodies. There Sir George obtained his trophies, and the black constables following helped themselves to other ghastly souvenirs. Amelia smiled as she watched them from the camp. So others too found male organs attractive in a morbid kind of way.

When the corpses had been flung beneath the overhanging lip of the gorge, Sergeant Barron found a method to dispose of them. He got a cask of gunpowder and set up a mine which, when blown, would explode the bank to bring it down. He was an expert at demolition and, when the boom came and the dust rose and settled, there was little evidence of the encounter that had taken place just that morning. Sir George was pleased, for the evidence had been destroyed and now only the official (his) version of the events would remain.

Amelia waited until things settled down, then stirred things up again. Her wails came from the tent where the body of the miner had been placed. Sir George hurried to her to see what other catastrophe lurked to trap him. He was relieved to find that the female was alone with the corpse.

'Poor, poor man,' she wailed. 'In the prime of life, only to be murdered by savages far from steppe and tundra. He was a Russian, wasn't he?' she queried. In her seeming agitation, she jerked at the blanket to reveal the corpse, whose face now was swollen and as black as any of the natives. But what held Sir George's attention though this time he was not after specimens – was the ripped groin and the dried blood. He stared long and hard and drew from it the inspiration he needed to put the massacre behind him. The grisly sight confirmed that it had been their Christian duty to avenge the foul deed. After all, did not the Bible speak of an eye for an eye, and so on.

Amelia waxed lyrically. 'This is the fate that awaits those men of the empire who settle at her very boundaries,' she wailed. 'Call Sergeant Barron, he who has saved you from such a fate and me from that other which women fear more than loss of life itself. Call him, to witness what he has revenged. They slaughtered without mercy and received none in return. O, O, to think that there are those who see such savages as merely dark forms of ourselves. O, where is the nobility in such creatures? I can't bear it. Such sights are not for womanly eyes'. And she shuddered and slumped in what seemed a swoon.

Sir George quickly replaced the blanket. When the others arrived, he stated: 'This day has been too much for the lady. Her senses gave way when she accidentally saw that act of barbarism inflicted on a Christian, though a Russian. One who never did harm enough to justify what has been done. Now, with the natives scattered and the remains of those who stayed left to the fire, let us bury this man in a befitting fashion. Hard is the road and hard is the time spent in civilising such savage lands. I shall myself perform the burial service so that Christian words ring out over this pagan land. Monaitch, the first of those to accept the Lord, bring me my prayer book.'

Sir George helped Amelia up and to her tent while Sonny, under the direction of Sergeant Barron who pleaded an old war wound which stopped him from digging, excavated a grave. After Sonny had dug down a few feet, he deemed it deep enough and took up the body of his mate and placed it therein. As he did so, the image of the giant nugget came into his mind and he could not escape the gleeful thought that it was now all his.

Sir George Augustus loved a religious service. In fact, once he had even aspired to the cloth, but alas, his poor education and background had denied him this. Now, he assumed the role of minister of religion and duly performed the funeral ceremony, keeping to the Established Church version, though before rising in the world he had been a Methodist. Still, that was past, and he flung himself into the interment and laid to rest the body of Russian Jack. After exhorting the assembled men, peppered with exclamations of faith from Monaitch, Sir George's last act was to place a hastily constructed cross at the head of the grave. As the constables began filling in the hole, he turned to see if Mrs Fraser had sketched the lonely and bleak service; but she was not there. He sighed, for she was not fulfilling her duties, though he had to admit that she had performed admirably in other ways. He fingered the Deed in his pocket and could not help thinking that the Russian's death had removed an obstacle from his path.

It was then that the woman called him. She had made tea for Sergeant Barron, Sonny (who alone was witness to the finding of the huge slug) and of course himself. They came together at the civilian tents, which were some distance from the mound of earth and the cross marking the lonely grave.

Amelia passed out the mugs of tea, then turned her veiled face to the police sergeant and said: 'Sergeant, you are a hero and saved us all today. Without you, the ambuscade would have succeeded. In short, they would have dispatched us; but if an inaccurate account of the battle got out, false accusations might be made. It is excellent that we have Sir George with us to put before that committee in London, who are only too ready to believe the worst of things, the true facts. How little they know of us pioneers and how difficult it is first to police, then to civilise and missionise a savage land. Thankfully Sir George, their agent, is well aware of the hardship of your lives and also of the labours that are necessary.'

'Too true, ma'am, too true,' Sergeant Barron agreed.

'Yes, yes,' Sir George exclaimed. 'I know the hardships and have partaken in them myself. In fact, I was one of the first free settlers to the island in the south. You are to be commended, Sergeant, and if I have my way your actions shall not go unrewarded. Believe me, I have the ear of the governor and if you desire a grant of land in a more salubrious part of the colony, I am sure that it may be arranged forthwith to your satisfaction.' His voice reached a semblance of its normal shrill tone as his enthusiasm rose. 'And here, and here, at this very spot where the forces of savagery and paganism were contested and defeated, here I shall recommend that a mission be constructed from which earnest missionaries may go forth to labour in the salvation of those who, as we have seen, are under the direction of the Devil. Satan walks these plains and verily they burn with his lust and ambition. He must be put to flight as those we fought today were put to flight; but that is not enough. I declare that what occurred here today was the aftermath of a tribal war, that black contended against black in a vicious slaughter and, when they had done with each other, the victors turned their animosity upon us, and so forced to defend ourselves we, in effect, revenged ourselves upon those who had already taken life. They have been punished and fortunate it is, for this area with its valuable water source is now free of them and ready for our occupation. Sergeant Barron, I, as an emissary of the government, order you to hold this place until the governor informs you as to its further disposal, which, I know, will be into safe hands able to stretch out in friendship to those survivors of the tribe which so viciously attacked us. Sergeant, see to it that this site is kept free of those pernicious fossickers. It is destined as a flourishing mission devoted to the salvation and upliftment of savage souls.'

'Well, Sir George, I don't know about that, it being a desolate place and all,' Sergeant Barron protested mildly, scratching at his moustache in perplexity. He had no wish to be stuck in a place weary miles from other humans. 'Not much to recommend it, apart from the water. Best I station my detachment at Yillarn. They need law and order there. It will be time to be here when the mission is ready to be established.'

'Patience, man, patience. It will not be long,' Sir George replied, his voice dropping from its shrill. The last thing he wanted was this area to be left open for any wandering prospector to fossick on. 'Be patient, stay here until your orders arrive,' he stated, and then made up his own mind as to his future actions. 'I will leave at once for the town to inform the governor of what has occurred here. A short report from you will serve to render my account accurate and this night I shall transcribe it for you. And, of course, I shall stress your bravery and appeal that it be rewarded. A grant of land – name your area and acreage. If there is to be a police station to be erected here, it shall be under your charge.'

'I would prefer the diggings.'

'Yes, later the diggings, Sergeant. This water source needs to be kept under our control for the present. And you, Sonny, you are experienced in the sort of establishment I wish here. Stay and be my presence on the site. Let no one loiter on it until other arrangements are in place. Son, you have my trust and I know that you will do this for your father.'

'But, but –'

'Sonny, I found you here and you may stay on a little longer. Do not fail me at this time.'

Sir George Augustus stared speculatively at Sonny and Sergeant Barron. It appeared that they would obey his instructions, at least until he and the governor had made other and more lasting arrangements. He felt that he could leave them to think over their future. Excusing himself, he went to his tent where he began constructing a short report which he would get the police sergeant to sign next morning. This flowed easily from his pen. He re-read it and checked the spelling against that of his Cambridge dictionary. Then, as his urge for composition quickened, he began a much longer report with a full description of the tribal war such as might have happened, and of the resulting bloodshed, which Sergeant Barron, under Sir George's direction, had quelled with minimum loss of life. He made notes structuring the middle portion, then wrote out in full the concluding sentence:

> It is a sad commentary on these natives; and as this account bears out, their lives are nasty, brutish and short. It is our Christian duty to rescue them from such depravity and savagery. It is, and I repeat, our duty!

CHAPTER TEN

'You are left in charge of this place. The civilian agent, so to speak,' Sergeant Barron observed, pulling at the peak of his kepi, then smoothing his moustache. 'Godforsaken place it is for sure, but the savages are no longer a threat, so I'll leave you for just a few days. As a police officer, it is my bounden duty to show the colours, as it were. We'll patrol as far as Yillarn, then swing back. Mount up,' he ordered his boys, then turned back to the civilian. 'Guard the camp and see to our draft animals, and the luck of the English to you.' And with that he mounted up and, at the head of his constables, trotted away.

A despondent Sonny stared after them. Alone again; but this time with a horse and cart instead of a schooner. Alone, as he felt he had been for most of his adult life. Well, he was used to it and damn them all. He remembered how his father had left him on the island and sailed off never to return, and how he perforce had had to grow used to solitude in which he could rave and rant without a single person to hear him. Memories came to him of his ailing mother, who at least had loved him when she had not been under the influence of her medicine. She also had left him too often to his own devices, or used him to complain of her ever-increasing ills and the absence of a husband who, when he did return, took them off to a miserable windswept island where she lapsed into a lassitude from which she emerged only to whinge before taking refuge in her medicine bottle; and so it had gone on, around and around with Sonny at the very centre. That island indeed had been a cursed place, though there was work enough until everyone had up and left, leaving him behind. He had loitered in the empty and decaying mission until he had managed to get to another island where they had pastured their sheep. A shepherd among his lowing flock, he had descended into misanthropy, being content with the company of his woolly friends; but that had been too good to last. His father had reached him even there. He had sold out the lease and others had come and evicted Sonny. Dispossessed and without a penny to his name, and not knowing where his father was, he had put the ship skills he had learnt under the direction of that black, Wadawaka, and joined a ship voyaging to Westland. Sitting in a tavern there, drinking out his meagre earnings, he listened and caught the gold fever; or rather he was taken up by it, for there he met Russian Jack who wanted him for the horse and dray he had bought to further his lot in life, perhaps as a woodcutter. Later, with most of the supplies already on the cart, they had had a falling out and Sonny had left for the diggings on his own. If the man wanted to keep up their partnership, he could find him there. The bloke came after him, gave him a thumping for going off without him, then they had pushed ·on into the desolation and at last came to the water at Kalipa. Now, instead of sea spray on his face, Sonny had dust, and instead of complacent natives, there were bloodthirsty savages who lurked in the bush – or used to, he reminded himself; for, thank God, they had been all wiped out. Every man jack of them!

Still, even a savage could do for company, though it was best to keep your distance. This his father had drummed into him, exclaiming how they were English and civilised, whereas *they* were – well, not. He only wished Russian Jack had kept his distance. Instead of sticking around when that girl came, Sonny had left him and, because of it, his mate had ended up a mutilated corpse. This last thought, with its accompanying disturbing image, caused Sonny to shudder and stare about him apprehensively. To his nostrils there came the pungent odour of burnt flesh. Was it the stink of decaying bodies from the gully where the blackfellows had been buried? His eyes flickered towards the collapsed bank, then looked out over the desert. In the heat haze, he thought he saw dark figures slipping towards him. He removed his wide-brimmed hat, wiped the sweat from his brow and focused his eyes. Nothing, just had the willies that was all, what with being by himself. He carefully replaced his hat, pulling the brim low over his forehead to shade his eyes from the harsh light.

To fill in the time, he saw to the horses. This took an hour or two, and he was left standing a solitary figure, before slumping to the ground as melancholia hit. He thought he had caught it from his mother, for it was when he thought of her that he descended into the gloom which reminded him of the semi-darkness in which she had kept her bedchamber. With it came the lethargy, and now he untangled himself and went to his tent to curl up on his swag. Great dry sobs racked his frame. He clenched his eyelids tightly together and blocked his ears with his hands. Now he moved the palms over his eyes and kept the fingers over his ears so that he was blind and deaf. Like some kind of sentient worm, he listened and looked within himself, first at his misery, then at a growing panic from which he rushed with a shout of 'Father!' Then, starting up, he bellowed: 'Mother!' Not even an echo. The flat land made his voice thin and reedy before swallowing it up completely. This was the beginning of the pattern and he went willingly into the old ritual. He fumbled in his dead mate's swag to see what he might find and came up with a bottle of rum still with half of its contents. He unplugged it and had a good long swig. It gave him the strength to leave the tent, which was too hot for him to bear.

Bottle in hand, he walked to the edge of the gully and stared across the desert. The flat expanse was not even broken by a hint of dust cloud. He uncorked the bottle, tilted it over his open mouth and let it run down his throat. The fiery liquor made its presence felt immediately. The sweet blow of intoxication hit the nape of his neck, then sent him back into his listless state. He sat, drinking, thinking of his dead mate and staring at nothing. What was there to see, or whom to listen to blathering on as that Russian Jack did? At least he had had his revenge. The smell of the charred bodies came to him, but it was rendered pleasant by his thoughts.

The bottle was soon emptied. He flung it away from him in the direction of the mass grave and pushed himself to his feet to stagger to the tent of Sergeant Barron. 'Bastard,' he slurred, examining the neat and tidy tent. Well, there it was. Barron had been using the small cask for a table. He picked it up and shook it. 'Slosh, slosh, slosh,' he chanted, then said aloud: 'Got to get me mug and fill it right up, brimming full.' He staggered back to his own tent for a pannikin. 'Slosh, slosh, slosh,' he chanted again, as he filled his mug, drained it and poured out another. Carefully, so as not to spill a drop, he wandered back to his spot in front of the gully.

'Bastard!' he declared to the desert. 'Ain't got no mother, no father, no mate.' He flung off his hat, felt the glare hit his blue eyes and pulled it on again. 'Bastard!' he shouted again, then: 'My kingdom, my kingdom for a … Gold!' he remembered with a sudden bellow. 'The nugget, the nugget!' he screamed. 'I'm rich and it's all mine, mine!' His lassitude vanished and his thoughts came wildly. He had struck it rich and could leave this forsaken place and go to the town. He tried to think about what he would do after that, and came up with a blank. He didn't know and perhaps did not care.

Sonny's enforced solitude with the sheep had wiped out whatever ambition or direction he might once have had, as had the domination by his father, leaving him like a ship bereft of sails and masts. Shrugging, he turned again to drink. It would give him direction. Now he must hold that massive slug of gold in his hands, caress the warm soft metal and feel that he had something all to himself, much as once he had felt that he had his mother's love. He lurched to his feet, staggered and fell down, got up, fell down again, reached for the pannikin for a drink, and this time managed to stay upright.

Using a long-handled shovel to steady himself, he made it to the gully lip, then slid down the bank to sit there staring at the stone under which they had cached their find. He crawled to it, pushed it aside and then scrabbled at the dirt with his hands. Nothing, nothing! He scratched away frantically. Nothing, nothing, nothing! The dirty natives had stolen his gold. Well, he would get it back and with this, his pistol. They must have hidden it at their camp.

Bare patches of round marked where their huts had been. He staggered from one to another, but the earth had not been disturbed and was baked as hard as rock, except for the covering of powdery dust with which he was soon covered. In his dementia, he attacked the funeral pyre. His shovel struck a half-burnt body and the stench made him gag. 'No nugget, no nugget,' he screamed, waving his shovel about in agitation, and to drive off the stinging swarm of flies that had risen from the ash heap. Perhaps he had been digging under the wrong rock. At a strange staggering lope, he headed back towards the gully. His drunkenness was receding as the enormity of his loss took over. He slid down on the seat of his trousers in a cloud of dust, brushed away the swarm of flies about his flushed and sweating face, then stared wildly along the bed. His spirits sunk. It had been the right rock. He wanted to curl up and die; but he merely sucked at the blood oozing from his skinned palms. Then he began to wail and followed it up by beating the ground with his bloody hands. At last, he retreated to where he had set his pannikin down on the edge of the gully near the demolished bank. Like a thirsty man, he gulped the liquid down. Another idea struck. Down he slid into the gully again, close to where the bodies of the slain natives had been covered by the slippage of earth. It stunk, but what better place to hide his slug of gold. He lifted high his shovel, almost losing his balance in the process, then plunged it down. There was a squishy sound and a slight resistance to the blade, then an eruption of evil gas that smote him in the face, so that his head jerked back as if from a blow. It was then that he glimpsed the pebbles – and his spirits soared.

He could hardly believe his eyes. He loosened his grip on the shovel handle and fell with it to where the explosion had shattered the underlying ancient sedimentary rock. The crater was filled with thousands of small shining pebbles. Reverently, he took one up between thumb and forefinger and rolled it between them, feeling the warm smoothness of pure gold. Gold. He scooped up a handful of the little blighters and tossed them from hand to hand. 'Strike, strike!' he yelled, his heavy boots jigging about in an ecstatic dance.

'Gold, gold!' he screamed, crushing the soft rock underfoot and revealing more and more of the precious metal. 'My gold, gold,' he shouted. 'Mine, mine!'

His thoughts tumbled chaotically about how to handle his sudden wealth. He would have to collect as much as he could and then cover up the deposit before the police returned from their patrol; but there was so much. He could load his dray with bags and bags of it, then be gone before they got back.

He dashed to the police carts and found some empty bags which had held fodder for the horses. Now, to get cracking and be off with his wealth; but to where? Of course, the town; but Father was there. No matter, go to the town and then decide what to do; but what did he want to do? Well, something would come to him and he didn't need a father to aim him in the right direction. In fact, that man would be the last to know of the find. He would only take the lot and Sonny wasn't having that. He went and refilled his pannikin. Since he was going, he could drink up the whole keg and damn that soldier who had never once offered him a drink. Stingy bugger, but who cared now? Well, he must get the sacks filled.

When one was a quarter full, he tried its weight and found that he could just lift it. He would have to reverse the process: take what he could carry and fill up the bags at the dray. He lugged the quarter-full sack to the cart, slung it up there, then went to his camp and found a panning dish. This would do to carry the pebbles of gold.

For the rest of the day, he went back and forth, the work stopping him from pondering on his future. Whenever he had a rest, the image of his father came ready to give advice; but the very thought of that person made Sonny hurry back to his task. He would not share his good fortune with him. No, he wouldn't, and he would avoid him when he reached the town. Once, when he had been lingering over a rum, his father had spoken one word, 'Sheep!', and Sonny had been given his future, though he had not realised it then. Father took the sheep away, just as he had taken everything; but he would never get this gold, never!

The sun sank and the moon arose to flood the desert with light. Shadows seemed to flicker over the plain and move towards the camp, but Sonny did not see them; that is, if there were anything to see. He sat at his fire, boiling up a mess of pork and beans; once, when he glanced up, he thought he caught a movement. Was it a kangaroo? He had never seen a single animal out here, except a few goannas and snakes. 'Fresh meat,' he said aloud, and grabbed for his pistol before deciding that his dead mate's musket would be better. He sighted on where he had seen the movement and fired. The harsh report shot off across the desert, but there was no reply, no sudden bound of an animal or a cry of pain to show the ball had struck whatever might be out there. He reloaded, taking his time.

His mind was as vacant as the desert and he had a spot of rum to help the thinking process along. Instead of madly gulping the liquor a he did when the mood was on him, he now sipped it pensively and gazed out onto the moonlit plain. Again, what appeared to be creeping shadows made themselves felt rather than seen. He stared long and hard until whatever might have been out there resolved into a flock of sheep, and he gave a shout as his father's imagined word came back to him. Why, yes, that was what he could do. Amongst his sheep he had been reasonably content and comfortable. He had liked that island too, surrounded as it was by an ocean which kept away intruders. It was cool and the air moved with the flow of the seasons, unlike here where the air lay inert on the land and shivered with the heat. Sweat and flies and emptiness. Whereas on his island his sheep moved over the downs and the winds blew from the west to bend the trees east.

'That's it!' he shouted. 'I will buy back my island and raise sheep and cattle and make cheeses and be content. I shall be king of that island and I shall name it King Island.'

In his excitement, he drained his mug of rum, then took up his musket and fired a shot across the plain in celebration. The ball hit one of the advancing shadows. There came an eerie scream of pain, then a wailing began from the direction of the gully. Sonny reloaded and fired his gun again, this time slanting the shot so that it went down into the wadi. The wailing ceased.

'Bloody natives,' Sonny muttered. 'You can't get rid of the blighters.' He refilled his pannikin and sipped on throughout the night. Nothing came to disturb him, even when he finally passed out and the camp remained unguarded.

CHAPTER ELEVEN

Sir George took only the bughi and a single dray with him, plus a change of horses for both, for he wished to make the best time possible. The black guide, Monaitch, drove the cart which was laden down with two tents and fodder for the horses. Behind the seat of the bughi Sir George had packed his provisions and also a package, closely wrapped. The journey to the coast was uneventful, a continual plodding across a featureless plain towards where a pall of dust hung over the land. This marked the diggings. Sir George camped overnight there, away from the massed tents. He did not even seek out the tavern, though Amelia took the opportunity to satisfy her thirst.

Early next morning, they were away on the rutted track, passing every now and again the remains of stripped wagons and carts. But although traffic had increased rather than diminished, they circled only one long line of men, walking and riding, and with these the knight exchanged only a few curt words. It was a slow and thoughtless passage through the barren plain. The worn horses moved slowly along, seemingly with their eyes closed, and even the dingo, which had begun the journey trotting beside the bughi, now lay curled up on the back of the dray. This relieved the knight, for on the outward journey the woman had persisted in having the animal, when it tired, lying beneath their feet. On occasion Sir George had been startled to find its great brown eyes on him, but when he had tentatively patted the animal, it had jerked its head away.

The wheels clung to the ruts. Sir George, who drove the bughi, merely had to hold the reins and let the horse have its head. In the past, he had been a loquacious traveller, regaling his fellows with accounts of his explorations and expeditions of pacification; but as on the outward journey, his companion, Amelia Fraser, clad in an all-enveloping forbidding black, did not invite conversation and appeared to doze the days away, though she regained her energy when the sun went down. Sir George put this down to the heat and the harsh light which she physically could not bear. Perforce he also became taciturn, constantly turning over in his mind his sudden fortune and how the discovery should be handled to his advantage.

When the silence became too much for him, he left the bughi, passing the slack reins to his companion, and joined Monaitch, the native guide. Monaitch was also at a loss for words, nonetheless Sir George sought to draw him out on the customs and curious habits of his tribe. Monaitch quickened when the subject turned to religion, and the knight was gladdened as he heard the fellow declare his faith in Jesus and the afterlife. Such a conversion, he truly believed, showed that the natives were not, as some would have it, beyond redemption but had merely been waiting for the preaching of the Word. This he now did with great effect, dredging from his mind long biblical quotations which he then explained in simple language to the new convert.

In this way, the journey continued at a constant pace, sometimes relieved by a sudden hymn from Sir George. At last, there began the scrubby vegetation which showed that they were approaching the edge of the plateau, from where they would be able to see the ocean and the town. He decided to camp right on the serrated edge where, hopefully, a sea breeze would dispel the constant heat which had begun to afflict him so that his rash had grown worse. Back on the south island, where the heat rash had developed into eczema which had continued to plague him ever after, he had treated it with a mixture of gunpowder and fat: a rank blend which had made him a comical sight. Now, however, as befitted his station in life, he used a soothing coloured ointment containing a tincture made from coca leaves which reduced the itching to tolerable proportions. Conscious that this was not available in the colony, he did not offer to share it with Mrs Fraser, who must also be suffering discomfort under her heavy garb, though she made no complaint. In spite of the ointment which numbed his skin, Sir George sometimes scratched at the pimples that disfigured his face. Once or twice he drew blood – an occurrence which his female companion appeared to observe closely; that is, as far as he could tell the direction of her gaze beneath her veil. But the attention, if it was there, stopped him from scratching and by the time the pass had been reached his complexion was beginning to clear up, much to his relief.

Now they were almost at their camping place. It was still light, but the horses were tired as the fodder was days gone and the scanty and dry vegetation along the road did not yield enough for them to keep up their strength. There should be better grazing for them at the plateau edge, which received more rain – when there was rain. Sir George slipped off the bughi to wait for the dray, noting with satisfaction the rather tall eucalyptus trees that grew there and the brush that covered the spaces between them.

As he clambered up onto the dray, he was startled by a loud voice shouting from the brush: 'Bail up!'

Sir George reached for the musket (his own pistols were in the bughi) which lay behind him, and found the woman's dog sprawled on it. Such an evil brute, he thought, with that sad way of looking at one that dogs had and this one in particular. Then all ruminations and groping hands were stilled. A pistol shot rang out and the whiz of a ball past his head made him desist. At least the damn noise had aroused the animal. It sprang from the cart and looked towards the bughi where its mistress was, raised its head and sniffed, then turned with a yelp to the undergrowth beside the track.

'Bail up!' shouted the voice again. A rider spurred his mount from the scrub and whirled it to a halt between the vehicles. He grabbed the bridle and jerked the cart horse to a stop. Then, as the bughi continued its slow movement forward, he galloped to it, reached for the reins, pulled on them and shouted: 'Whoo, whoo!' Swinging his pistol around from the heavily draped figure there, he levelled it at Sir George and his blackfellow and commanded in a gruff voice muffled by the colourful bandanna which completely covered his face: 'Get down, or else I'll blow yer down.'

Sir George stared at the pistol which had twin barrels and thus still held a load. The highwayman had another stuck through the sash that kept his dark cloak closed about him. The knight obeyed. He was puzzled, however, for even though the voice was muffled, there was a familiar ring to it, and Sir George prided himself on never ever forgetting a voice. In fact, having started out with a cockney brogue, his rise up the social ladder had necessitated a change of accent which had meant a study of voices, and this is where his skill had come from. What he found even stranger was that the woman's dog was wagging its tail beside the horse.

Traitorous brute, he thought. If it had kicked up a commotion he would have been able to get at the musket. He jumped down and stamped his foot as he demanded: 'Fellow, what is the meaning of this?' He glared at the draped man and shrilled out: 'We are on the Queen's business. I am not some merchant you can overawe. Give way, or by God, I shall see you hanged.'

'Hanged be damned!' the man shouted back. 'I am past the caring.'

The dog squatted on its haunches and calmly regarded Sir George, whose eczema had turned a bright red.

That damn dog – and that voice? The knight stared hard at the man, but he was dressed in similar fashion to Mrs Fraser, with not a patch of skin showing. A broad felt hat was pulled hard over his eyes so that not even these were visible. Strange, Sir George thought, was the aversion to the sun catching? 'Enough of this tomfoolery,' he blustered. 'Enough of this pretence at highway robbery. We have nothing of value here for a ruffian to plunder. Give way, give way and let us pass.'

'Give way indeed when you have a laden cart, and that means a toll fee if you wish to use my track. It belongs to me by right of conquest and is held by force of arms. You as an Englishman must know that force makes right.'

It was then that the voice and tone evoked in Sir George a flashback. A vision of the schooner which he had finally gotten from the government after a barrage of letters; and with the vessel had come a person, a convict no less, to train his natives in the crewing of her. And not any convict, but an insolent black from Africa who, even though he had been a slave, was not afraid to answer back. 'You fellow!' Sir George suddenly bellowed. 'You are the African convict. How come you here?'

The dog whined as his mistress hopped from the bughi. 'John Summers,' Amelia called. 'It is you, isn't it?' she said with a laugh. 'And a highwayman too. Fancy that. And so we meet again.'

'Amelia,' the robber replied, put out by her presence. His pistol quivered to her satisfaction.

'This is my dog, George.' She indicated her animal. 'He seems to be glad to see you – but I am not.' And she called her pet to her.

'And, rascal, you remember me, for you were under my command,' Sir George grated.

'Fada, the buckra,' the highwayman said promptly. 'We meet again, but now I am a free man.' He waggled his pistol, adding with a harsh laugh: 'With this to defend my freedom. This, sir, is my highway, so give over or you shall be brought down, sir, as the Devil is my witness. And there she stands.' He gestured towards Amelia with his pistol. She stroked the dog's head: her only reply to his insult.

But Sir George was outraged. 'I always knew that a rope would be your end, and I shall see to it directly,' he said sternly, his voice rising again to a shrill whine. 'How can you escape when I have the ear of the governor? What is more, I am now no longer in command of a dismal native settlement, but a knight of the realm and a magistrate. Your offence is a hanging matter. Those who live by violence deserve to die by violence. By God, I shall see you kicking –'

'O pshaw,' Amelia broke in. 'This is the famous John Summers. I knew him in England when my father took his case, and I came to succour him when he languished in prison without family or friends. He – we – fought to free the slaves in England. You know me, knave, don't you ... and your promises to me?' she said in too soft a voice for comfort. The dog caught the menace and whined and slumped down from under her caressing hand.

'Yes, I know you and that is enough knowing. You are a *subaga*, drawing out men's promises along with their wits, then you do them ill.'

'Such ingratitude,' Amelia observed to Sir George. 'I took food from my own table to feed him when his fate was to be Jamaica. Remember that island in this quotation: "We stood on the square at the harbour. There was a cage in the middle of the square. We heard the wind from the ocean, the harsh rustling of the palm leaves, the brushing of the palm fronds used by the Negro women to sweep the dust off the square, the groans of the slave in the cage, the surf. We saw the breasts of the Negro women, the bloody weals on the body of the slave in the cage, the palace of the governor. We said: This is Jamaica, disgrace of the Antilles, slave ship of the Caribbean Sea." A delightful fate, indeed, and this is the thanks I get. He deserves the rope, or worse, this, this example to his people.'

'Base ingratitude deserves such,' Sir George retorted. 'Fellow, you have been identified twice over: surrender and face manfully the fate you have brought upon yourself. Or are you to add to your crimes by murdering both of us? Surrender,' he demanded. 'Benefactors have laboured for such as you.'

There was a silence, broken only by the snuffling of the dog. Amelia bent and stroked its head. Monaitch said softly, 'Hallelujah,' as they all stared at the highwayman, who had been unmasked as it were. Now, to protect his identity, he would have to kill them all.

But John Summers, also known as Wadawaka, was not the callous reprobate they accused him of being, and the mention of the slave isle had rekindled within him his pain. His brave stance fell away as he slumped in the saddle and replied in a voice which had lost its strength. He murmured: 'Murder both, do I include the black and make it three? Then there is the dog which knows me. Murder, enough of the talk of murder, from those with blood upon their hands and lips. Her eyes burn through that wretched cloth. A nightmare! Old Buckra Jim's nightmare on his return to his mission, to find the slaves in control and he bereft of all and destined for rags. It is like that for me, but why, why?' Then he straightened up and said in a deep voice, which unconsciously mocked Sir George's shrill: 'Murder, bloody murder. To live answer me this: do you know the white-necked raven?'

Sir George exclaimed: 'What is this nonsense? Throw down your pistol this instant!'

But the black highwayman raised his voice to reply: 'I know you and your works and you must know the answer. A would-be preacher and missionary who came to me in that prison, drowning me in your ideas of God and redemption, until I believed you and became your captain as you plotted to profit from those poor wretches under you. And here is another question: how many survived your ministry? Answer me that!'

'Long ago, when I was over the likes of you,' Sir George screamed, setting his listeners' teeth on edge. 'Better to be dead and saved, rather than alive and damned as you surely are.'

It was then that Amelia broke in with a chuckle: 'I wondered why Sir George wore a white stock and a black frock coat when I first met him, though now he wears light cotton cloths and a wide-brimmed hat which makes him more like a planter. Is he that Jim Buckra? No matter. I wondered why I never sought his blood. It is too vinegarish for me.'

'It is the answer. Those who go around with a white stock about their neck and a black coat on their back, creating dead bodies to bury. This one here has buried many.'

Amelia laughed. 'He certainly has and that not so long ago. But be careful, he does a lovely burial service ...'

Sir George shouted in exasperation: 'What is this nonsense? Are we to bandy words with a common criminal? The rope for you, you rascal. The rope, my word upon it, and I shall indeed read the burial service over your dead body. The schooner was left in your charge. Return it!'

Amelia replied to this in a soft voice meant only for the knight's ears. 'How many were massacred, Sir George, and did you conduct a burial service for them?'

'Well, what of it? An attack was repulsed. We defended ourselves against a savage onslaught. Tribal war –'

'But, Sir George, would the House of Commons committee now examining into the treatment of the natives within the empire accept your version of events when there is mine to place against it? Need I say that my father is a lawyer, one who is active in such philanthropic pursuits? He defended this man here when they sought to keep him property within the kingdom.'

'Beware, woman. That was years ago and he is surely dead,' Sir George shrilled. 'Beware. Those who sought my reputation lost their own. I have friends and am a knight of the realm and an expert in my field. But what is this man to us? We have other business to conduct, let him be on his way. Passing acts of sympathy do not create a lasting bond, especially when we have a shining future to consider.'

'Please, Sir George.' Amelia suddenly began to placate him. 'We are of like mind; but if one helps a living person to remain alive and free, do you then desire him dead or a slave when he uses his freedom to – well, in his case, to play the highwayman? He is, I know, somewhat headstrong, but sturdy in morality as well as physique. Why he seeks to earn a living in this poor way is beyond me, especially when we, with our cargo, need a worthy champion. What I mean is, we could use him as a guard –'

'No, for he was once under my control and now he is on the rampage. He shall always be as he is, and there is the matter of my schooner –'

'Schooner shmooner. Who cares, now that you can buy a hundred of them.'

'This, this utter scoundrel! An escaped convict and now a highway robber.'

'But strong and able to guard us. A scoundrel is better than an honest man in our business. Invite him to join us, he is in need of succour and we have more than enough on him to have him kicking in the air if he goes against us.'

Sir George blustered about the impossibility of having such a man about him, and base ingratitude, and would have continued long in this vein had not Amelia gone close to him. The sun dipped low in the sky and shadows held the track in thrall. She lifted her veil and stared into the man's eyes. Suddenly he gave a start, looked about him in consternation and said: 'Why, it is time to set up camp. The head of the pass is near. You, fellow, have held my attention, but it is for the better. We need a sturdy arm to guard us. You, I take into my employ – the conditions we can discuss later – but first be rid of that absurd cloak and bandanna. I do not hold a grudge, but see that you serve me well.'

'And me, and perhaps the dog as well.' Amelia laughed.

The ex-highwayman shrugged his massive shoulders and said: 'Witch. But to haunt a stretch of desolate road is perhaps worse than his employ.'

With that, he sighed long and deeply, then clambered from his horse and divested himself of his cloak and bandanna to stand there in his rough seaman's garb. The dog bounded forward to lick his hand, but Amelia regarded him from a distance, her face screwed up in seeming disgust. His hair had been closely cropped and his face shaven. He was very different from the man she had known and taken as her mate. She stared at him overlong, drinking in his features with her memories of being cast off. With a hard expression on her face which belied her words, she murmured: 'Poor man, if I can call you that, you have been through hard times. But then so have we all, and when I look at you I see debts to be paid and, by the Devil, they shall be paid and in full.'

The man busied himself with the dingo and refused to reply. She glowered at him, then called the animal to her. 'You know him,' she gloated. 'He is a pet and I like pets.'

Sir George stared at the cloak, bandanna and pistols, then gestured to the African to pick them up and pass them to him. 'These,' he said, 'will stay with me. Today was an adventure, sir, and I shall remember it. It will make an interesting episode in my projected memoirs, though there is still that other volume on native habits and customs to consider. But, no matter, or does it matter? And that horse, where did you obtain it?'

'It is the governor's. It was the best on offer.'

'And the accoutrements, I suppose they belong to the governor too. What are we to do with them?'

Without replying, John Summers took off the saddle and then the bridle. He dumped them beside the track and slapped the horse across the withers. It trotted off a little way, then stopped.

'I doubt that it will gallop off,' Sir George observed. 'If it follows let it, for I will return it to the governor, but its trappings, let them remain at the roadside. Someone will find them and either return or appropriate them as he wills.'

He turned and was about to get into the bughi when John Summers said: 'There are more of us, some of those you used to call your sable friends.'

'More Africans here?' Sir George exclaimed as if wonders would never cease.

'No, remember the mission,' the African replied wryly. He gave a low whistle.

Old Jangamuttuk – looking even more ancient than Sir George remembered him from his time as emissary to the natives on the south island – came out of the undergrowth. He was attended by another black, Hercules, who was clutching a huge club. After them came Ludjee. Yes, it was indeed her, his Lalla Rookh. Now she grinned at him in glee and exclaimed: 'Fada, you left us alone on that island and we been looking all over for you. Now we together again.'

'Oh my God,' Sir George exclaimed in return, aghast at being confronted by his past, living and breathing.

'You gave me that powerful name, Hercules, Fada,' the giant blackfellow bellowed, wagging his club, then bringing it down ·upon the ground with a thump that made the knight jump. 'I keep the name along with the story. He had a club and now I have one too. You told me that he wore the skin of an animal called a lion, but I am still looking for that fellow to get his coat. I kill it just as my namesake did,' he shouted. Again he brought his club down upon the ground, startling the horses and making the black guide, who had been wondering where these strange blackfellows had come from, bounce in his seat.

'And here I am.' Jangamuttuk spoke last of all. 'Your old sable friend. Fada, how could you leave us? But we have found you at last, thanks to Wadawaka here. Did you enjoy the joke he played on you? Ludjee, she thought it would amuse you. Bet you were scared, eh?'

'Yes, it was a fine joke,' the supposed highwayman said, 'but I did not see that woman hidden under the hood of the bughi. If I had, I would have been far from here. She is evil and hard to keep in check.'

'Easy for you to say,' retorted Amelia. 'You took everything, then tried to evade me. Well, like a counterfeit coin you have turned up again, and now see if you can leave.'

'My God, you enthralled and tortured me, now you play the victim. Hard was the fleeing and swift was the return. Well, keep yourself to yourself, we know you.' He turned to the knight. 'We have passed through difficult times: many died and the schooner failed to survive.'

'Looking for you, Fada, looking everywhere,' Ludjee wailed.

'Here, there and everywhere,' Jangamuttuk said in his turn, though he was squatting and talking to the dingo who appeared to be listening. How it wagged its tail.

'Even under the ground, just like Hercules and I saw that great big dog, that Cerberus, and gave him a good thumping. There was lots of meat on his bones. Not only that, but –'

'Yes, yes, yes,' Sir George muttered, nonplussed, put out by the appearance of those who knew about his misdeeds. He could not help but thank Providence that they were black and thus at a disadvantage if it came to their word against his. Moreover, he was a knight and an author, and what were they? What were they indeed, and he smiled, for as once he had used them so now he could use them again. They, after all, were living proof of his success at civilising such creatures. He remembered how well the troupe of Iwoway Indians had been received in England, even being granted an audience with the Queen, and how he had wished then that he had had the foresight to bring some of the natives of this far land back with him. Now he had the means and he visualised himself in London at the Anthropological Society, surrounded by the members who seemed not to have taken kindly to him. He had wished for a seat on the governing committee but had been unable to garner enough support. With a group of these blacks, that could change. Yes, it could, and he rubbed his hands in glee as he got his vehicles underway.

CHAPTER TWELVE

At last, coolness. A soft breeze blew, laden with damp sea air, as Sir George ordered the camp to be set up. Monaitch pitched the tents while the other blackfellows made themselves useful building campfires. One for the knight (whom they persisted in calling Fada) and the other for themselves at a distance from the tents. Now the guide busied himself preparing Sir George's meal. Amelia (whose dog had deserted her to be with his mother and friends) strolled along the serrated edge of the plateau in order to avoid being asked to partake in the meal. To her right, on the coastal plain, the lights of the town glowed, and in the harbour a long line of lights moved up and down with the waves. Except for a cursory glance, she took no notice of it, wandering along to where a dark gleam revealed where water had collected in a crevasse. It was fed by an underground river making its way to the sea. She pulled off her heavy constricting clothing, stretched leisurely, rubbed her breasts, then waded into the pool from a small beach of tiny pebbles. She swam about, then began scrubbing herself with bottom sand. She ducked down a few times, then emerged, glowing white in the darkness. She picked up her heavy clothes, which were stiff with dust, and bundled them up, all except for a shift which she put on before going back to the camp site.

Sir George had had his meal and a lantern glowed in his tent where he was hard at work writing. His sable friends sat about their fire, finishing off their meal – some sort of gumbo or chowder which the African had put together. Amelia stared at the figures huddled there, before flinging her bundle into her tent and going to them with a grimace on her face. There, she confronted the African who had betrayed her, or who at least thought he had, for his expression changed to one of wariness as she stood before him.

'So, you left me alone and unaided while you ran away on that ship. I watched you desert me and now you come creeping back. Well, explain yourself,' she said in a hard intense voice, glowering at him with frightening reddened eyes. He avoided her gaze; his glance flickered over her body. The clinging shift showed her to advantage, but to increase the effect she moved to stand in front of the fire. Now he might see her body outlined, though her face was in shadow. She smiled and said: 'Well, been about the empire's business, have we? Me trapped safely underground while you are free to go and play with fishes. Did the nasty big white beast scare you, so that you had to come running back to mummy? Well, she's good and mad and just as bad a white beast.'

The black man looked up at her face hidden in the shadows, then dropped his gaze to her hips as he declaimed: 'Hard was the sailing and hard was the chase –'

'O you Africans, with the gift of the gab and the legs of a gazelle. Well, you've been run down good and proper. Don't frown, just relax with your mates and give them a yarn. I expect they're waiting to hear your adventures, and I will bear it for a time, until I remember how you treated me.'

With a sigh, the man fled into words. 'The gazelle is an anxious animal and easily frightened, as is the leopard for all his claws and fangs. As for the human, well, he has invented ships to sail the seas. It is as much his nature to do so as it is for a deer to panic.' His eyes left her hips and drifted off into the darkness as he began his tale. His body began to sway, as if he were again on that ship. 'If an African can sweet talk you into calmness, then Americans can move you into their obsessions. Such a strange vessel; such a strange skipper. A Yankee who lived only to kill the white whale. They called her Moby Dick, believing that only a male could wreak such havoc, whereas I dubbed her *The Empire*.'

'So we're into symbols now, are we?' Amelia retorted, even stamping her foot. 'I expect that captain saw in her, in that Moby Dick, more than a monster that had eaten his leg. Well, go on, if the tale can bear the telling.'

'He did rave and rave and ranted so much that I guess he did see her as a symbol of his loss. He signed me on as a harpooner and I found myself a savage among savages held in thrall by a savage skipper. Ahab was his name and he clutched a Bible in his right hand, a pistol in his left, blasphemy in his mouth, and in his heart hatred for that sea beast. Lord and master over us, he drove us along with his phantasies which he thrust into us poor savages, whom he believed alone had the nature to hunt down the creature. I, too, came to believe this as my fellows regaled me with stories that refused to accept the monster as a blind force of nature, but one filled with all the cunning of the so-called civilised; in short, the empire which rules our lives as surely as that Moby Dick ruled Ahab, sending him on a morbid chase across the seven seas. I ran from you; but all of us, including our gaunt captain, were also fleeing. He saw that in me and so took me aboard.'

'Yes, fool, I had already escaped that silly trap that old shaman there caught me in. This land is underlain by channels,' Amelia said, at last sitting down. 'And so I stood and watched your flight into an obsession worse than mine. Yes, I stood there and let you have your sea voyage. What cared I? My life is long and I have the time to indulge your phantasies.'

'Yes, I saw your dark figure and the sight of you made my aim true. I struck the mast and Ahab's heart. He made me a harpooner to be with the savages that echoed his own soul. Such a rum lot. There was Queequeg from an island to the east. He was tattooed with the intricate tracings of his clan, which when one stared hard enough resolved into the writhings of an octopus. He slept with a juju doll, an ancestral skull from which he took the future, as well as a tomahawk which doubled as a pipe. He smoked some concoction and kept on puffing away, filling our quarters with the reek of it and our heads with the fumes. He said that the smoke was an incense to keep the devils at bay, though it failed to work, for he was foretold his future death by that skull. And he fashioned a coffin made by the ship's carpenter who laboured long, fearful of both savage and tomahawk. Ahab oversaw the work and when it was finished hung it at the stern to show that death was the due of all. Then there was Tashtego, a native American, for so he styled himself. In short, a Red Indian, much like these who listen to my tale. He was the last of his people and, having had enough of those who had pillaged his land, had taken to the sea to aid them in pillaging the waters. At times, he moaned in his sleep and once he told me that in his dreams he was hunted through the skies by that great white beast for his soul. Now he hunted her earthly form to redeem himself, for, once she was killed and despoiled, he would be made whole and his people would spring up again proud and strong. The last, apart from me, was a fellow African, Daggoo, who had never been a slave, except under whaling captains such as Ahab who treated him better than the masters of the plantations had me. He stared long and hard when I first came aboard, took in my ochre locks and stance, then decided that all of us on this far land must be of the same race as he. Daggoo, too, was obsessed by the beast we hunted and needed to slay her to put an end to the nightmares of his dreams, which had begun when he left his native shores, going aboard a ship that sailed off never to return. In killing the beast and in bathing in the sweetest oil from the very skull, he believed he would find his homeland again, though he scarcely remembered it. So we four each had a purpose in slaying that great white monster which mocked us with her invulnerability; though we believed we could kill her, what with being under that Ahab who had the necessary guile and magic to bring her alongside dead.

'But he was insane and so our voyage was insane. How to describe it and what it did to us, poor savages all, who, roused by Ahab, existed but to do the deed? He, forsaking charts and maps for his own intuitions, linked his mind to that whale and both hurried us to our doom.

'We followed after through the ragged oceans and finally she let us come up to her. I was with him that day, in his lonely boat which laboured through the waters as the crew heaved on their sullen oars. Only Ahab and I, the harpooner, had common purpose. The crewmen wanted only her oil and ignored the vendetta with which the madman and his savages were polluted. Tashtego, Queequeg and Daggoo held the three mast heads. Aloft, they swayed in ancient rhythms, their eyes and voices cursing the monster fish as her plume marked her running before our boat. They shouted as she began to slow. We hurried to her side, rushing through waves littered with the darting heads of sharks which snapped at our oars so that the blades became jagged, shedding splinters as they thrust into the waters with a heave-ho.

'"Pull on, pull on. Aye, pull on, we near him. Take the helm, let me near, I need to have at him," screamed Ahab, stumbling forward to the bows of our flying boat to perch like an ill-omened vulture, his pegleg steady in the hole he had bored for it.

'She let us come alongside her massive white flank, not deigning to notice us or the vulture perched upon our bow. We entered the smoky mist which, thrown off from her spout, dimmed the day with a certain solemnity. Ahab, with a gleeful and mournful shout, as if he was about to sacrifice his only child, reared himself up with back arched and both arms highlifted for the thrust, then, anchored by that ivory leg, flung himself forward, his arms coming down to dart forth his fierce iron; though, to tell the truth, for I watched from the stern, he seemed to hesitate at the last, so that the harpoon hung for a single eye wink, before it plunged down and deep into that cursed skin of whiteness. He shrieked as the line sizzled past his leg as the beast reacted to the sting.

'Moby Dick, as Ahab termed her, sideways writhed, rolling her right flank against our bow so that the boat canted far over. If it had not been for his leg, Ahab would have been flung into the sea. As it was, three of the crew were sacrificed as the monster charged the sweltering waves. Our line went taut ... and snapped!

'"What breaks in me? Some sinew cracks! – 'tis whole again; oars! oars! Burst in upon him!" So roared our besotted captain.

'But we were lame, and the whale, wheeling round to present her blank forehead, saw this, as well as the nearing dark hull of our mother vessel. It was a larger and nobler foe, and she turned from us and bore down on the advancing prow, smiting her jaws amid fiery showers of foam.

'Ahab sought to follow after, but the whale-smitten bow ends of two planks burst through and our boat was level with the waves. We bailed her out while the monster sped towards our ship. Tashtego was nailing to the masthead the red flag which betokened that we had her under chase, though rather she had us. I saw his hammer hesitate as the monster descended upon him.

'The ship's bows were hung with seamen, their enchanted eyes intent upon the kill. Now she raced in on them, strangely vibrating her head to send a broad band of overspreading semicircular foam before her. It reached our vessel, which rose and fell into her swift vengeance. The solid white buttress of her forehead smote the ship's starboard bow and men and timbers reeled. Some fell flat upon their faces; the heads of the harpooners aloft shook on their bull-like necks. Shouts and screams began as, through the breach, the waters poured as mountain torrents down a flume.

'Diving beneath the settling ship, the whale ran quivering along its keel, then, turning underwater, swiftly shot to the surface again, far off the other bow, but within yards of our boat. For a time, she lay there quiescent, content with her victory.

'Ahab darted in again his harpoon. The stricken whale flew forward; with an igniting velocity the line ran through the groove ... ran foul! Ahab stooped to clear it, and did so; but the flying turn caught him around the neck, dumbed him first, then shot him away. Ere the crew knew it, he was gone. Next instant, the heavy eye-splice in the rope's final end flew out of the stark empty tub, knocked down an oarsman and, smiting the sea, disappeared into its depths.

'The horror of it all drove me away from the human to the animal. I became my totem, a snarling leopard, but what could I do against such a monster fish? I rose high into the sky above our stricken boat and flew to the sinking ship, where only the arm of Tashtego showed above the waters hammering fast the useless flag. I swooped to him, hoping that he would rise with his senses; but all that I received was a slighting hammer blow that made me cease from any thoughts of rescue, though I continued to circle the submerged vessel, spellbound by her doom. The arm stopped its mad hammering as the flag dragged its sodden length beneath the waters and I glimpsed a huge form undulate away from where small fowls flew screaming over the yawning gulf which marked our ship's fate. I skimmed lower and saw that it was a huge octopus speeding forth after the white monster. I followed above, until it turned an eye on me. I knew that it was Queequeg when his voice echoed "adieu" within my head. His dreaming creature had been the octopus and he had assumed that shape to carry on the battle. He sped on through the seas after the monstrous white beast, but he was on his own, for .I had had enough of such a rampage. Moreover, another voice bade me turn and make my way back here. What else could I do? As I left, I spied the coffin bobbing on the waves. And that was the last of that sea voyage.'

'It was about time too,' Amelia retorted. 'I was growing bored with all that men's business. You and I are attuned, and where else could you retire to after she, tired with your antics, put an end to them? While you were adventuring on the high seas, seeking an end to the domination of a great white brute you called Empire, I was at my wits' end, so much so that I lost them and went darting through the endless tunnels beneath this land, which are enough to frighten any bat. If you wish for pallid monsters, try there. You could have hunted them as easily if you had stayed with me there, after I had guided you beneath the ground and sought to show you its wonders. Leviathans, giant serpents that block the tunnels with their bulk and with gaping mouths that seem but the continuation of the tunnel's length. I too had my share of monsters, but evaded their snares as I fled, bereft of you, down through the rank tunnels until I came up and up and into a cave which is not far from here. There, while I waited for the sun to descend, I traced out on the walls the handprints of victims whom the natives had left there to placate their demon serpents.'

Monaitch, who had been listening in bewilderment to the African's story, though he had enough English to follow the outline and to catch Amelia's words, suddenly shouted that the handprints were not the marks of victims fed to the giant serpents, but merely the signatures of those who had tested their courage by staying overnight in the cave. 'Those snakes *waugal*,' he told them, 'and once they lived upon the earth. Then went underground to make those tunnels. Link up all the waters in our country. That what they say, but now Jesus come into my life, what such things to me? I never seen one.'

'Well, you thank the Lord for that,' Amelia replied sardonically. 'They are more than enough for any god to handle, and as for the tunnels ... Only a bat could find its way through them. But, to finish off: when the sun at last left the sky, I came from the cave to find nearby the camp of a missionary and his wife who were seeking a goodly spot from which to convert fellows such as yourself. Well, they found another conversion and one not to their liking. After those tunnels, I was parched with thirst, thirsty enough to drink a missionary and his wife dry, be their blood as sharp as vinegar. I also needed clothing and she was of my size and height. The good lady wore only the deepest black by day, but by night the whitest of white. This is her shift that I have on. It still smells of lavender which might be the perfume of sanctity.'

Thankfully Monaitch, who had been converted by those missionaries, did not understand all of what she said. Ludjee did, and this reminded her of the nature of the thing before her.

'Poor things, to come across such an evil monster as yourself,' she declared. 'Once, I had you in my power and I should have put an end to you; but I am not a killer, though now might be the time to do it, for I know my blood sickens you since I am of the sea and not of the land. I, too, like my husband, am a shaman with a shaman's powers.'

'Yes, and once I had you in my grasp,' Amelia retorted, 'though I was somewhat upset at the time. If I had not been, I might have devised a different ending to you and overseen it properly. I tried, and thought I had done you in. I saw you change and change as your flesh boiled away. How is it that you still live, or are you a shadow from beyond?'

'You saw what you wanted to see in your demented state. When you observed the steam over that underground waterhole and the bubbling, you thought that it was boiling hot; but it wasn't. Beneath the surface, a hot and cold stream met and I changed into Manta Ray, my totem creature, and swam along the cold stream beneath the rocks, enjoying the coolness after the tepid warmth of your underground nest. There were tunnels flowing with the sweetest water and I sported along them, not seeing any serpents. I thought that in time I might meet the ocean and regain my strength; but it was not to be and the water, though cool, leached away my magic. I became a human and had to escape up into the cavern where I sought my husband. It was bare and empty, and if I had stayed there, I too would have been driven mad, for I lacked the power to escape.'

'But deep underground, far from the sun, I increased in strength,' Amelia gloated, 'though the great rush of energy made me mad. And then again there is that old blackfellow, your so-called husband. He was never without a song or stratagem; but how is he here? He evaded me by changing into a rock, plugging the hole so that I could not follow after my dog and my lover-husband. Why isn't he still that rock?'

'And that's another thing. That dog, as you call him, is my son and you have charmed him away from me. Now he is at your beck and call, but I want him back. I told you once to leave me and mine alone, and you failed to heed the warning.'

'Pshaw, what can you do to me? You are a silly old woman with a senile old husband. I smile at you, and as for my dog, ask him. He wishes to be with me. Later, I want to know how that old man escaped. Shaman or no, it was a difficult task.'

Hercules got their attention by thudding down his club.

'I was there when they needed me,' he boomed. 'Did not my namesake descend underground, and where he goes, I follow. That big dingo – one blow and he was dead. I used his meat for provisions and went down to that river. There I came to the ferryman, who saw my club and held his tongue. I flung him a piece of meat and he took me to the cavern. There I came across Ludjee searching for her husband. I strengthened her with my meat and we found this boulder lying on the floor. It appeared to have fallen from a great height, for part of it was embedded in the rock. I pulled it out and flung it from me. Lo and behold, there was the old fellow lying there asleep. A tap from my club was enough to bring him to his senses and we returned the way I had come. Another piece of meat and that ferryman bent to my will.'

'I was having a good rest, trying to get back to the form of my totem creature, Goanna,' Jangamuttuk chuckled. 'Then I found myself flying through the air and suddenly I was struck. See there, that bump on my head? It still remains. That thing there had gone, but it was nice being a rock in that ceiling, nice and cool.'

'Pity you didn't stay a rock,' Amelia observed. 'But don't blame me, for it was that African who wanted a sea cruise.'

'It was all your fault, all of it,' Ludjee retorted. 'Another word from you and Hercules uses his club. If that doesn't fix you, I'll try something else.'

'It won't.' Amelia laughed and licked her lips. 'If he wants to, let him try. I like big fellows, though my husband might not like him attacking me.'

'Enough of old silly things,' Monaitch broke in harshly. 'They gone now and with them Devil's magic. Jesus has come to this land. New magic in the air. Look, look, down there on the waters. A sign, a sign! He has come to save us all in that big ship, all made of iron, but it floats. What are giant serpents and whales beside it? How powerful Jesus is! Look up, there in sky, see! He has marked it with his cross sign.'

'His sign? No, it isn't,' Jangamuttuk exclaimed. 'That is only the beginning of the road leading to the milky ocean. I followed it when I took those of my people from the wrecked ship and led them up there where they might rest, free from the ghosts. I left them there, and when I have completed my journey to the west, I will follow after and we shall rejoin them. So it is and it has nothing to do with Jesus. I and Ludjee continue on down here. I, the Master of the Ghost Dreaming, declare it to be so.'

'Old man,' John Summers replied, 'the world is round, as round as a ball, and if you continue west, you will arrive back where you started. Is that what you want to do?'

'Well, let it be, let it be, there is still enough west for me, and I shall attain such things that when I return to where I began I shall be wiser than all of my people put together. And if the world is but the serpent eating its tail, I shall see my own land again, check out those places I need to, then leave when I'm good and ready.'

'But you are alone down here, except for Ludjee, Hercules, and perhaps the dog, though he is different from you.'

'And you, Wadawaka, and you, perhaps this white thing too. When the time comes, I will know who to take with me. And that iron ship down there – I have brought it here. It is for us and has nothing to do with that Jesus, unless that Fada is Jesus, for he comes along too.'

The shaman began to clap his hands rhythmically and to chant under his breath while the others stared down at the town and the low row of lights moving up and down in time to the eternal rhythms of the sea. Suddenly, the light in Sir George's tent went out and they heard him sigh as he turned in.

'Well,' Amelia observed, 'be that as it may. Time for bed too, though the night is mine and I have this so-called husband to work my wiles upon. Such a big, strong man, but look how he cowers. You know, I can't hurt him. He does not belong to the land. Fancy it, from black slave to black gentleman to black savage to whaler to highwayman and then back to John Summers. Who, I wonder, must he think he is?'

'Why, he knows. Wadawaka, of course, Seaborn. Who else could he be?' Jangamuttuk declared.

'Of course, who else?' the African agreed, yawning a great yawn which denoted tiredness of spirit as well as body. He saw before him his ocean and felt the movement of the waves beneath him and their surge within his mind. 'Yes, Wadawaka, Seaborn,' he said with another yawn. He got up, hesitated, then extended his hand down to Amelia.

She spurned it, jumping to her feet with a scornful laugh. 'You were too long on that ocean, Seaborn. Wasn't there a cabin boy? I don't trust you. I wonder whether you would be here if you had killed the great white brute, or would you have gone back to Nantucket or wherever they paid out your wages?'

'Really, I embellished my yarn,' Wadawaka replied in order to placate her. 'In truth, it was but another whale to me, to be strung at the side of our vessel and relieved of her oil while the sharks snapped up the red flesh of her body.'

'Oh yes, to believe you is to believe in Moby Dick.'

A voice shouted: 'Monaitch, you take the first watch. Be on guard now and don't let me catch you sleeping.'

'The master calls,' Wadawaka said bitterly, 'just like old times.'

'Well, he has magic,' Monaitch declared. 'I his guide. He promises to make me policeman.'

'Once he tried to order me about,' Jangamuttuk said. 'Do this, do that, and all I did was go off and keep away from him. Him and his Jesus. Well, we all have a bit of Christ in us.'

'Blasphemy, blasphemy!' Monaitch shrieked. 'I tell him and he preach to you good and proper, save you from darkness of despair.'

'And from things that go bump in the night,' Amelia said with a laugh. 'I'm one of them, you know.'

'The Lord is my shepherd.'

'And I'm one of the things that live in the sea,' Ludjee exclaimed.

'Be not afraid, He declared.'

'And I fly through the sky,' chortled Jangamuttuk.

'I stalk the land looking for my lion,' declared Hercules.

'He leadeth me from temptation. Heathens all.'

Again the querulous voice of Sir George sounded: 'Enough of this chattering. I want to make an early start tomorrow.'

'I could finish him off,' Amelia suggested. 'Give him a little bite from the darkness.'

'Let him be,' Wadawaka said. 'They are as they are.'

'Yeah, let Fada be,' Ludjee said. 'Once that Fada was good to us. He gave us that schooner, didn't he?'

All except the black guide laughed.

Jangamuttuk said: 'That Fada, always making those marks on that thing he calls paper. Maybe I'll learn that magic next. Might come in handy.'

Monaitch, empowered by being in the employ of Sir George, spoke up: 'Time to sleep.'

He went to the dray, found his musket, shouldered it as he had seen the constables do and began marching up and down in front of Sir George's tent.

The African sighed as he looked at him.

CHAPTER THIRTEEN

After sleeping the sleep of the dead the night of his return, Sir George rose out of the arms of Morpheus to find his bed empty. This did not faze him: his wife must have become accustomed to loitering about the bungalow while he had been on his arduous trip, though now he was back she should have been there to help with his toilet. His wig needed a good brushing. Grumbling at her lack of consideration, he recovered his good humour only when he unwrapped the huge slug of gold to gaze lovingly upon it. He extended one stubby finger to trace out the curls which had caused him to name it the Golden Fleece. In fact, as he fingered the metal, he felt like Jason of old: he too had gained his prize at the expense of some lives; but what matter, as long as it was put to profitable use? Now he must keep his appointment with the governor and ensure that his land grant of Kalipa was firm and fixed for all time. As it was an official meeting, he dressed accordingly. After pouring water from the jug into the basin and dashing it over his face and bald head, he, overconscious of his naked dome, jammed on his wig before opening the chest which contained his dress suit. He tut-tutted over his linen which had lost the snowy whiteness which befitted a gentleman of distinction and means. Some sort of fungus had attacked the neat stitching and extended out to tinge the rest pale yellow. It could not be helped, nor could the creased and crumpled condition of his dress coat and trousers. His attire suggested a status below that of a gentleman and was close to what he might have worn years ago when he was conciliator on the south island. But, far different from those days, there lay his *piece de resistance*. He carefully wrapped up the slug of gold and cradled it in his arms. So heavy and so massy, so unignorable.

Clutching his prize to him, the power of the nugget filling him with satisfaction, he strode forth to meet the governor. He set his package down, knocked on the drawing-room door and, on receiving permission to enter, bent, heaved up his bundle again and passed through. The man, for once, was seated at a desk, though still held the inevitable glass in his hand. Sir George smiled at his slovenly dress. The years in the colony had affected the governor adversely, lessening his concern for sartorial splendour. He wore a semi-military jacket with tarnished buttons and, what was worse, let it gape open to reveal linen – no, Indian cotton decrepit with age, and was it dirt? Sir George thought that he had nothing to fear from such a person. He waited.

The governor glanced up at the knight, cleared his throat, glanced down at the dusty papers on his desk and then at his glass. Sir George observed him wryly. It was not exactly the place for an office, but this would be rectified in time when the mines began producing. Then the new government house would rise majestically as a monument to the new status which he, Sir George, had bestowed on the colony. He bent down and carefully placed the package on the wooden floor.

'Ahem, Sir George,' the governor muttered, 'of the illustrious house of Augustus, a Roman emperor, no doubt of that at all, and I trust, I know that your, your expedition has been all that it might have been. You contacted the savages which infest those inland areas, which I have heard are barren wastelands, dry and as raspy as this damn collar is.' He tugged at the collar of his shirt which was already gaping wide enough to slip another neck inside.

Any reference to Sir George's origins made him extremely uncomfortable, for although he was proud of being a self-made man, he was also sensitive to the fact that he lacked the pedigree to be fully at ease in the presence of a member of the ancient and illustrious Crawley family. There was, however, the consolation that he had researched the governor and his wife, for to be forewarned was to be forearmed. The governor was all that he claimed to be, but his spouse was not only of dubious origins, her mother being an opera singer, but also of reputation. Scandal had necessitated the then Colonel Crawley of the Coldstream Guards accepting his post here. All in all, this was to Sir George's advantage.

His discomfort eased by his reflections, he smiled as he took the seat indicated, a cane chair of Indian manufacture. It creaked under his weight, though he was a small person and his stoutness had been sweated away by his sojourn in the desert. He was past his prime, but held his age well, well enough to have gained a young wife for a settlement of only two hundred pounds per year. He thrust such thoughts away as he turned to the business on hand.

'Colonel, Your Excellency,' he began, patting his head to ensure that his wig was on straight, for his discomfort had returned. He observed the half-empty glass on the desk and the circular impressions which many similar glasses had left on the desktop.

'Ah, yes,' the man said, noticing his eyes on the glass. 'Yes indeed, all good things come to those who wait and I have waited months for this brandy. Try it, it is excellent. Drink to your success. Wine, sir, is hard to come by, and when it arrives swiftly turns into an amber liquid of an undrinkable nature, though I believe that Hindoos sometimes use it as a medicine.' He chuckled and topped up his own glass before dashing some into another. 'From the large ship, sir,' he observed, pushing it with his fingertips towards the knight.

Sir George gingerly took it up, noticing the dust particles floating on the surface. It was too early in the day to partake of spirituous liquids but, unwilling to cause offence, he sipped, found it decidedly of superior quality and took a gulp.

'Sir George, to your health and to your success,' the governor said, raising his glass and taking a large swallow without waiting for the knight to raise his. 'Now to business. The draft of the land grant met with your approval? Good, good. Missions and suchlike alleviations for the savages go down well in London, and here too, as long as they are far from the town. Perhaps you can take the lot from here. They are pests, content to laze about the harbour front, though I have forbidden them the streets after sunset.'

'Providence has given us this land to civilise and control,' began the knight. 'It would be a shirking of our duty and His command. But you said a draft of the land grant. I took it to be the legal Deed itself.'

'Yes, yes, yes, the Almighty, eh, and His plans. Some of us are more privy to them than others. Plans, indeed. Thousands of acres' worth and far from us. Yes, a worthy project, herd them there and keep them there, especially now when hordes of men flock to the colony for the precious metal. More reports, sir, that is what it will mean and some of them must concern the natives. Yes, yes, a worthy project, one that will go down well in London when you speak of it.'

Sir George decided that the governor was befuddled and humoured him. 'It shall, Your Excellency, it shall, for it is well known that when a lesser race comes into contact with a more powerful one, it is the lesser which goes down. I assume that the grant will be as I wished it?'

'But not at government expense, sir. The colonial office is adamant that colonies must pay their way. They query every penny spent.'

'It is the new government, Your Excellency, and the South African business which cost a pretty penny is over. I assure you that I expect no government funding. Subscriptions will be taken up to alleviate the plight of the inhabitants. That is, if they are necessary; for there is a further fact which I now impart to you in strictest confidence. Your Excellency, the mission land is gold bearing. This is beyond doubt, but as those fossickers are too near, it must be protected and I have taken the necessary steps. I have left Sergeant Barron and his native constables to guard the future mission site. What needs to be done and quickly is to set up a police station to patrol the goldfields. Law and order must be maintained and private property protected; and under private property, I include native land which we must hold in trust for them. Why, on my return, I was attacked by bushrangers and had to fight my way through. A strict policing is absolutely necessary and a licensing system must be put in place, Your Excellency. There are some hundreds of men there, and soon there shall be thousands.'

'Yes, yes, and to the detriment of the colony, for the town is almost deserted except for women and children. Sir, our labour force is gone and these natives, although slow to take to work, are being recruited to fill the gap. We need more settlers, but you are against convicts, so where are they to come from?'

'There is no need of them now. The lust for gold will cause immigrants to flock to the colony. But, fossick as they may, they will soon learn that the exploitation of our mineral wealth requires more than picks and shovels. Your Excellency, heavy machinery as developed on the Californian goldfields is needed, capital is needed, railways, and a constant and plentiful water supply. And so, a person of some importance is required to advertise the prospects of our colony in London. Your Excellency, I am that man!'

'Yes, yes, money and machinery, steam engines and waterpipes, and your good self soliciting them for our future benefit. What more do I need, but a clerical staff to oversee the development? Work, work, nothing but work.'

'But the rewards, consider the rewards! Clerks, you shall have. When the news reaches London, what recruitment there shall be, and even if they abscond when they arrive, they will soon be ready for work when they find the better claims under our control. Our future as to population is assured; it is the capital we must find. Down here there is water enough and if a weir or dam be built, a pipeline may be laid to where it shall do the most good. Then the railways. In other colonies a scheme has been devised: land in exchange for the laying of the lines. There is enough of this, and enough in faraway London of those who shall know the quality of such.'

'Yes, yes, such great, though tedious possibilities,' the governor muttered tiredly, his hand going to his glass. 'All this and more, but not at present. Sir, at present there are few indeed to perform their duties here. Have you observed that massive vessel anchored in the harbour? It brought five hundred bodies to flesh out the colony, and, sir, all are on their way to the gold strike. It was difficult enough to get her unloaded. Why, even the sailors might have absconded if I had not placed a guard along the harbour front to deter them. Such a huge vessel to be stranded here might mean my recall; but all is well, as the captain assures me. She shall sail the day after. The master is to take dinner with us this night and you may attend to hear the latest news from home.'

'And the vessel is to proceed directly to England, Your Excellency?'

'She shall steam back to Southampton to take up the Atlantic run. This has only been a proving voyage. She is the largest vessel afloat and, if she proves herself, she is but the first of many.'

'But on the return voyage, where shall she find cargo and passengers?'

'Passengers and cargo are of lesser importance and would but delay her. The owners seek to establish a record to prove the swiftness of their vessel. She shall sail all but empty to the Cape colony, where she shall take on coal, for she needs a deuced amount of that, and perhaps find cargo and passengers there while she coals, then on to St Helena where more coal has been stored, then a straight run to Southampton.'

'Your Excellency, I feel that this vessel in the harbour has been placed there by Providence for our benefit.'

'What the deuce, man! It was to benefit us with an addition to our workforce, now it is a hulk as empty as the town.'

There was a flurry at the door. It opened to let Ludjee through. Sir George examined the servant he had given to Government House so that she might regain the civilised habits he had once instilled in her. The woman was dressed in an embroidered shift that had seen better days and carefully carried a silver tray laden with tea things. The china was exquisite and the teapot, tea strainer, milk jug and sugar bowl were of silver. The remains of past splendour, Sir George thought, as was the lady, Mrs Rebecca Crawley, who followed. She had dressed for tea, though her attire was years out of fashion as evidenced by the crinoline, and the climate had rumpled and battered the finery. Still, she carried herself well, as befits a lady, and her opera singer of a mother had passed over a flair for costume that would show through even if she wore rags. She regally directed the native woman to place the tea things on the sideboard.

Both men got to their feet on Rebecca Crawley's entrance.

'Well, a native servant who seems to know how to carry a tray without dropping the whole thing or slopping the tea. Things are starting to improve, I can feel it, and perhaps it is because of our famed guest,' she said, dimpling her cheeks in an expression which age and the colony had rendered to a travesty of what once had been charming.

'Yes, they can be trained to serve adequately,' Sir George agreed with a smile. 'In my position as commandant of an institution for their betterment, I found that it was possible to instruct them in certain menial tasks. This of course was done by my lady wife, who alas succumbed to the rigours of life in that colony.' His smile vanished and a doleful expression sat on his face.

'Ah, but she was soon replaced,' Mrs Crawley observed with a smile.

'Madam, it is written that man and woman are but halves, and wholeness must be maintained. This I sought to do by taking a second wife, though naturally, my first spouse, the mother of my heir, holds first place in my heart,' he pontificated, thanking God that the son was far from him.

'Gentlemen, tea is ready so please take your seats about the table. Including you, my dearest one.' Mrs Crawley curtsied mockingly at her husband. 'The poor dear is either tied to that desk or that chair. His work, you know.' And she raised her eyes to the ceiling.

Both men went to the table and Sir George continued.

'What is needed,' he said with a fervent air, 'is a missionary couple to oversee their training. This I will recommend in my report, and I am sure that funds will be found to send such a pair out and to support them in their endeavours.'

'How I wish that I were in London,' Mrs Crawley replied just as fervently. 'When I was there I was on all the charity lists and I would hold a fancy fair for such poor benighted creatures and even serve at a stall myself. Just look at this poor woman here. She needs to be clothed properly, but who is there to do that? It is beyond me. All that I could do for her modesty was to hide her nakedness beneath that shift. It does not become her, or myself as her mistress. How terrible, creatures of the female sex, roaming about without a stitch on them. I shudder at the thought.' And she grimaced, daintily casting down her eyes demurely as she murmured: 'Though, I confess that I am fast approaching that condition too. Such costumes, sir, I am forced to wear. Why were we not informed of the coming of that vessel? I would have placed an order with Moses for some more appealing apparel, though it would be ready-made and I hate to wear such things. Still, since my dear husband is here, then I too must be. It is only right and proper for a wife to be at her husband's side, even to the extent of depriving herself of everything she holds dear.

'How I suffer here, more so when I peruse the periodicals from home. I have been glancing over a journal which came with the ship and it appears that there is to be a great exhibition in London. All the world will be there, except for my poor self.' She sighed and began pouring out the tea. 'At least the good captain has provided us with some luxuries from home. Thanks to him we now have these dainty biscuits, as well as the excellent brandy my husband cannot leave alone. Please have one, Sir

George, and you too, Your Excellency,' she added mockingly. 'They will not last.'

Sir George nibbled at his biscuit, then lifted the dainty teacup in his pudgy fingers and essayed a sip. His little finger poked out in what he considered the approved manner. He took another sip, then said almost to himself: 'An almost empty ship, a soon-to-be exhibition in London and a worthy object to place on show. I trust that the colonies will not be excluded?'

'I confess I did not read that far as yet, but stopped when I saw that His Royal Highness, Prince Albert, is the worthy patron and then I was lost in memories, for more than once I was fortunate to meet that goodly prince, who (it is written) saved the project by his enthusiasm,' Mrs Crawley replied, then added with a shrug: 'But what could our poor colony show to the world, except those dirty naked natives?' She pulled a face, glanced at Ludjee and indicated the door.

'Yes, the natives,' Sir George said. 'Why not? They could put on some of their rude dances – under my supervision, of course, to ensure that they are in good taste; but that is only part of what we are to display. Your Excellency and you, kind lady, it is time to unveil what lies within the interior. A precious object which will be the cynosure of all eyes and bring flooding in the wealth we need for development. Prepare yourselves.'

Dramatically, he got to his feet and lifted, not without effort, his package onto the desk. He untied the cloth and there lay the Golden Fleece.

'There,' he exclaimed, 'there is our exhibit. Who could resist?'

Mrs Crawley's eyes grew feral with greed. 'Huge,' she exclaimed. 'Gigantic. Enormous!'

'It is indeed,' her husband said, less enthusiastically. 'And pure gold from what I can see, though I had little enough idea when Bailey found that ore. I take it that it is from the grant of land which is in process of being transferred to you, sir? If there are gold nuggets of this size lying about, what must be beneath the surface? But if I am to set aside the area for the savages, might not this interfere with the exploitation? For, once missionaries get it into their heads to settle on a piece of land, the deuce you have to remove them.'

'Your Excellency, I must confess that the mission is only a subterfuge so that we might control access to the area. After all, it will not be gazetted solely to house the civilising processes; but even if it were, the natives might prove to be the labour force necessary to mine the metal. All is in our favour, for we are in possession and need only set up a company among ourselves, not only as a commercial but as a philanthropic enterprise, so that no one can accuse us of wantonly driving the natives away. There has already been a battle between two savage tribes, one of which held native title to the land, and they have been so decimated that the area is as bare of inhabitants as it is of vegetation. It is truly a *terra nullius* and is under my control through Sergeant Barron, who in future must be rewarded for his competence.'

'This does partake of subterfuge, for if the natives have all but wiped themselves out, how may a mission be justified, or the philanthropic aspect of the enterprise be stressed?'

Sir George struck a lecturing pose. 'Your Excellency, there are always natives when you need them. In my report on my great work of conciliation on the south island, I stressed the need to collect the inhabitants together for their own benefit. This report was widely quoted in the metropolis and it is readily acceptable until a better comes along.'

'Yes, yes,' the governor agreed, 'your work is well known and as you are here to report on the condition of the natives, there will be no problem in getting your views accepted. When a missionary comes, as one will – well, there is land enough not too close by and savages about the town for him or them to preach to.'

The governor had not touched his tea. Now he got up and went to the desk, lowered his head intently to survey the slug of gold, then poured himself out another brandy. His wife was fascinated by the largest piece of gold she had ever seen. She followed him to the desk, poured herself a large drink, then stood before the nugget.

'I have named it the Golden Fleece,' the knight said.

Mrs Crawley took no notice. Slowly, she extended her slim fingers to caress the slug. 'It is beautiful,' she said, 'so beautiful in shape and size, and it is all ours.'

'Well, not exactly,' Sir George exclaimed. 'It is the property of he who found it; but then I am ready to lend it to our purposes. See it not as a possession but as bait to entice industrialists with capital. It is lure enough, is it not?'

'It is indeed,' the woman breathed, her eyes alight. 'It is indeed.'

'And where was it found exactly?' the governor asked, eyeing the thing with some trepidation. Over the years, he had settled down in his job and reached the nadir of life that the colony provided. He lacked all ambition for wealth or advancement and could think of nothing except the stuff and bother which would result from such a discovery. He sighed, but then perked up. His partiality to indolence aroused in him an urge to profit from the discovery so that he might continue it.

Sir George, staring at him, decided that the question had probably been rhetorical. If not, he evaded the need for an answer by taking a leather pouch from his pocket and declaring: 'This is a small amount of what we might expect to obtain. I give it to you as a gesture of good faith in our future relationship and belief in developing this colony.' He upended the pouch on the desk and a scattering of nuggets spilled across it.

'More, more,' the governor's wife breathed, putting down her drink so that all ten fingers might touch the pebbles of gold. She toyed with them, her eyes growing hard and shrewd as she contemplated a future so wealthy that no one would ever again question her antecedents.

'Well,' Sir George said, having made his point and overcome the wife of the colonel. She was his and with her came the governor. He covered up the huge slug of gold, saying as he did so: 'No word of this must leak out until the nugget is on display in London. It would create a run onto our land which we might not be able to control, given the few constables we have there.'

'How could I breathe a word?' Rebecca whispered, her hands scooping up the pebbles; but her eyes lingered on the package.

'And it must not be put within your current report to the colonial office in London until events have superseded it,' Sir George added, getting to his feet. Excusing himself, he took up his load and left the room, so pleased with his reception that he quite forgot about pressing for the Deed.

'That man is not to be trusted,' Rebecca Crawley exclaimed as soon as the knight had gone. 'He has the eyes of a fox.'

'Well, dash it,' her husband protested. 'He seems honest enough and is cutting us a stake in the future. He could have pressed for the mission and hidden everything from us.'

'He is too cunning for that. He is sure to strive to keep the controlling interest.'

'Well, I have sanctioned a grant of land where the nugget was found and the Deed is ready. It is the best way of transferring the land from the Crown to private hands.'

'It is into whose hands that worries me,' his wife exclaimed. 'The Deed of Grant must be amended.'

'But I have given my word.'

'Your word! And what has that ever got you? This place where we rot! Now let me think. I have it: the land shall be deeded to both him and me, which means you, for the Married Woman's Property Bill still hangs in the balance. So, my dear husband, we shall safeguard our share by ensuring our share. Your word shall not be broken either, only amended.'

'Perhaps,' the governor replied, filling again both their glasses. 'It just seems a dashed amount of trouble. You see to it. It is in your hands.'

'It is indeed, and I will play on his susceptibilities so that he will accept the change,' his wife retorted tartly, her face twisting in seeming anger. 'I am right, you old fogey,' she added with a laugh, going to him and putting her arms about him, then lifting his head with a hand under his chin and planting an excited kiss on his lips. 'Pshew, you smell of brandy, and after this one so shall I. But this is the last, I have work to do. Soon we shall be drinking the choicest wines and liquors; for now, linger over your brandy while I redraft the Deed to our liking. Thank God he accepted as legal the one I did before. It lacked the official seal. I left that off on purpose and well that I did. And while you sip, there is something else you might ponder. Lately, I have had a longing to see my son. I miss the dear and last night I found myself crying, imagining him bereft of a mother's presence and love. And then there is that exhibition. Ah me, fortune does not come to those who hesitate; one must go and grab it, my old sweet love. How dashing you looked in your colonel's uniform. Do you remember when we first met? Ours was a love match made in heaven or hell, in spite of your rude old aunt and her aversion to me. Such wonderful times, until they dried up in this wretched place. No gaslights, no fashions, no carriages, no billiards, cards or old regimental cronies. Ah, London and soon the Great Exhibition, and my poor boy bereft of a mother to escort him there. Still, you are in the service of Queen and country ...'

'And expect to remain so for now, though the pay is as wretched as the colony. But there is a stillness here that puts me beyond such frivolities. I wouldn't know what to do with a card, or a cue for that matter, these days.'

'Oh yes you would. Once learnt and tasted, they are always there, and if all succeeds you shall have money to squander rather than debts to pay. No, let me nibble at that old moustache of yours. It still tickles so. Now I'm ready to do the Deed. Agreed, his name and mine? Good! It must be, for we still need him. It can't be helped, but we do. Now sip on your brandy and be quiet, my old one. Don't drink too much, for as the Americans say, I've got a hankering for you after seeing the size of that nugget.'

She gathered up the small pebbles into the leather pouch, then sat down at the desk and put pen to paper. Her husband sighed, but she was too busy to notice. In spite of all, the world had come rushing in to seize his wretched refuge by the scruff of the neck to tug it into the modern world symbolised by the monstrous hip in the harbour. He sighed again and sipped at his drink. It had been so peaceful here and now that peacefulness was going. 'Railways and steam engines indeed,' he grunted. 'What a lot of blather.'

My Dear Lord Steyne, or should it be Your Grace, for though we exist each to the other in letters only, your missives have become so scanty of late, that I do believe that our relationship has become formalised. I suppose it is because of my being in exile at the ends of the earth, though only through the small fault of having trusted you and helped in furthering your projects. Poor, poor little me, bereft of goodly company and with an ahemming and ahawing sort of husband who only snores beside me and seldom indulges his fancy, that is if he has any left. But I assure you that, even far from fashion and with only the rude lights of native fires to illuminate my darkness, I have not forgotten your kind patronage, though the efforts of enemies, both yours and mine, have made a pretence of separation too real. So be it, or as the poet says: 'Alone and palely loitering', though here is the rub and a goodly caress along with it. There is news indeed to impart and perhaps you shall deign to hear further from my own sweet lips if and when I reach the fair metropolis, which I hear from just-arrived journals is in the throes of mounting a giant exhibition of the nations. This I would dearly love to see. I have kept my side of our bargain for some years now, even to the extent of almost perishing from boredom. I feel that out of sight is now also out of mind and that those who maligned us have moved on to other subjects for their spite, or that the years have withered their concern and that the exposure we received is as forgotten as a novel of vain proportions which one reads then discards. After all, a certain Charles Dickens has lately risen to literary prominence and his subjects are far below us. So much has changed in Vanity Fair.

So be it, the sands of time are running and, as I pen this, my eyes alight on a great iron ship in the harbour. As she fills my vision, I feel that her arrival is opportune; but there is more to my wishing to be in the metropolis and at the Great Exhibition than may be gleaned in scanning these lines, which by the bye will travel along with me on the vessel and initiate the resumption of contact between us. This is necessary, for though we receive the journals late, it appears that recently – which in our part of the world means some months ago – you suffered a series of reverses of South Sea Bubble proportions; but all is not lost, or if you have recouped your losses then you have cash to set out for a goodly return. What I intend to say here in my poor way is that, my dear Lord, there is gold here. Yes, gold, gold, gold, enough to make your eyes glitter and glimmer, as mine did when I beheld a nugget of massive size, tens of pounds in weight and, what is more, the area whence it came has been secured by the buffoon I mentioned in my last letter and my own self through my somewhat scatterbrained husband. The former is clever in a London hackney-cab-driver way and, as for the latter – well, need I recall to mind how he never noticed the horns growing on his head until he became a victim of the plot to sever us and bring you down? Yes, Your Grace, my Lord, the gold is here and from all accounts merely needs the capital to delve after it. We hold the land and have posted a detachment of police to guard it from those fossickers who are flocking about our find and grubbing in the dirt without a penny to dig deeper to expose the hidden veins of treasure.

So much for this news, and news it is indeed. You always remarked on my cleverness and cooperation, and thus I feel certain enough about our mutual feelings, at least in regard to the golden wealth, that our meeting will be fortuitous for both of us. By the way, the golden slug has been named, aptly I hope, the Golden Fleece.

So, Your Grace, I bid adieu until we meet.

Rebecca Crawley

CHAPTER FOURTEEN

The rap-rap of clapsticks broke the silence of the evening and reached out to enter the seat of government. Rap-rap rap-rap. In the clearing which had been cut out for the new governor's mansion – separated from the bungalow by a narrow belt of scrub and trees yet to be fully cleared and thus left in a state of disarray – fires erupted to glow through the heavy boles of the eucalypts. The flames grew in size, as Jangamuttuk chanted: *'Fire, flickering, flame grows, flame grows.'*

Rebecca Crawley was dozing next to her husband when the sounds of the clapsticks came into her slumber. Under the stimulus, she stirred and a smile appeared on her sleeping face. The rhythm transmuted into the opening chords of *The Magic Flute* and she relived one of her triumphs. In a ballroom, a Grecian tent of fine linen had been erected within which a tall and stalwart man reclined on a couch. Above him hung his helmet and shield. It was her husband asleep and bereft of ambition as always. He lay there without a care in the world. A lamp cast the broad shadow of the sleeping warrior flickering on the wall, the sword and shield of Troy glittering in its light. The band played a melody from *Don Juan,* one of her special favourites.

A man stole in, deathly pale and on tiptoe. Behind him a tense face looked out balefully from behind the arras. There she was, ready to hazard all for love and revenge. The man lifted the dagger he carried and held it poised over the sleeper, who turned in his bed, opening his chest as if for the blow. The assassin hesitated, unable to strike the noble slumbering chieftain. She as Clytemnestra, queen and soon to be murderess, glided swiftly into the tent like an apparition – her arms bare and white, her flowing hair dark ripples to her shoulders, her face deadly pale with intent – and her eyes lit up with a smile so ghastly that people quaked as they looked at her. She exulted in her power and her deed. Scornfully, she snatched the dagger from the man's hand and raised it over her own head. It shone in the glimmer of the lamp. As the blade descended, the light went out. From the darkness came a shuddering moan.

Rebecca turned on her back, then sat up, still under the influence of the dream. She had been perfect in the charade and when Lord Steyne had observed: 'Mrs Rawdon Crawley was quite killing in the part', she had laughed, gay and saucy, and swept him the prettiest little curtsy that had gaped her bodice so that the tops of her breasts were seen to advantage. 'Those were the days,' she murmured, becoming conscious.

Jangamuttuk too was recalling the old days, during which in such a ceremony his consciousness slipped into another realm; but this night it shifted merely into the past. Visions of the first potent Ghost Dreaming ceremony drifted into his mind. *Once, Morning Star shifted in her course and the gateway was open. Once, Morning Star strayed from her course. She continued to shine, but left the morning for the evening. Now she shines marking the entrance far to the west from whence they come. I, Jangamuttuk, Master of the Ghost Dreaming, am travelling to that land. Our misery lies there and our souls are tugged there. Our spirits, they roam in a land whose very plants and animals, insects and serpents, wither and suffer.*

But such memories, although of suffering and sadness, lacked the depth of emotion to plunge him into the trance state. He stared up into the sky where he saw the campfires of the mass of his people who had escaped there to wait for him to come to them. All in good time, he thought. How their campfires flickered. Were they watching this ceremony? He chanted the next verses with more feeling:

'They made of me
A ghost down under.
Gave me a dram
It tasted like man
Flesh of my flesh,
Real as this dream
Way down under.'

The verses reached Rebecca together with another long moan. She stretched, daintily yawning, not wanting to leave her dream so abruptly, then came fully awake as she realised that all that was past and here she was in a dreary present right at the end of the world where there were no charades nor even important people to compliment her on her charming acting. And what were those rude noises from the bush and that moaning close by? She was about to waken her husband to complain of both, then put the idea aside. She could not bear the thought of her husband at the moment; but what could she do, now that she was wide awake and likely not to get back to sleep that night? Sweet slumber was a fitful friend these days. She listened to the sounds again and decided that it might be somewhat pleasant to spy on the savages and their rude and perhaps indecent behaviour.

Jangamuttuk began to sing in the language of those he still considered ghosts.

> 'They made of me
> A ghost down under,
> Made for me
> A place to plunder,
> A place to plunder
> Way down under.'

He finished the verse and began again, picking out individual words.

> 'Made me made me mad
> Ghost place ghost face,
> Ghost ghost, under plunder.'

A fit of coughing ended the verses.

Sir George Augustus, the well-known expert on the natives of the Great South Land, had always enjoyed their simple dances, especially those which employed mimicry. In fact, he was devoting a long chapter in his slow-coming book to them. What he professed not to like, and heartily condemned in public at least, were those which might be indecorous if not downright indecent. As the master now of his own performing savage troupe, he would have to oversee their dances, putting on only those which would entertain as well as educate an audience. They would have to rehearse them too, if they were to make an impact at the Great Exhibition. Still, all in all, what performances they did do would show the civilising process. Now, as the sound of clapsticks reached him, he decided to go and observe once again their rude revels in the natural state.

> 'They made of me
> A ghost down under.
> Gave me a dram
> It tasted like man
> Flesh of my flesh,
> Real as this dream
> Way down under.'

As he heard Jangamuttuk's voice chant, Sir George fell into a reverie of when he had last heard the melody. About a dozen years ago, no longer than that, and what a harridan of a wife he had had then. Thankfully, she had died just before the voyage home, leaving him as an eligible widower still within his prime, available to marry this angel of a girl who would never ever murmur against him for indulging in such simple enjoyments as observing the savages at play. How peacefully and innocently she slept beside him. Even when awake she was so uncomplaining and uncomplicated. Such a sweet, sweet thing, he thought, sighing over her sleeping face. He decided not to awaken her and left the bed, stopping only to replace his nightcap with his wig before stealing from the room.

Outside, he pulled on his boots and made off across the ruins of a garden which was slowly going back to bush. Such an impact gold had on the minds of men that the gardener-cum-servant had absconded from his duty. This was another proof, if one were needed, that the sight of the enormous lump of gold would draw forth the greed of men and, with it, the loosening of purse strings to release the flood of capital necessary to develop the colony. The observation put Sir George into an even better mood and he strode away from the house without a backward glance. Thus he missed seeing his young wife drift out of the room and, like a phantom, glide along the verandah and into Amelia's room. The door swung ajar behind her.

> 'They made of me
> A ghost down under.
> Gave me a dram
> It tasted like man
> Flesh of my flesh,
> Real as this dream
> Way down under.'

The words, and in English at that, drew Rebecca from her bed. She picked up her clogs – French of course, but still so ungainly in comparison to the footwear she had been so used to, necessary as they were in a place where no pavements existed. Their hardness and utter practicality almost made her fling them away in disgust but, unwilling to rouse her husband, she forbore. Slipping out of the door, she pushed her small feet into them, almost shuddering at their solidity. Then her good humour asserted itself. She smiled, running her hands over her body, feeling the soft material of the clinging nightdress. It covered her from neck to ankle and was decorous enough for the deserted night. She could not bear to put on the hideous corset and thick dress which so restrained her free spirit. She sighed as the soft moaning began again. It was coming from one of the guest rooms: Amelia Fraser's. Her curiosity aroused, Rebecca stole along the verandah to find the door ajar. A faint glimmer of candlelight came out.

She peeped around the door and saw a scene of depravity which thrilled her. Who would have guessed it of that ninny? she thought as she stared in fascination.

Lucy lay stretched out and naked on the bed. How white her body was; how dainty her breasts, how rosy-tipped; how slender and helpless her form. Her hands were tied to the bedposts so that she could not defend herself even if she had a mind to, for they were her moans which Rebecca had been hearing on and off for some time. Her legs also were tied to the bedposts so that they were spread wide apart and between them a young native lad knelt, pounding away at her twisting body.

'No, no,' Lucy moaned as her body bucked and then grew still.

Such a sight alone would have been scandalous diversion enough for the governor's wife, except there was more. Sitting next to the girl's head was Amelia Fraser, also naked and gleaming pale in the candlelight. When Lucy grew still, the woman, so white as to be almost ethereal, reached out a hand and twisted the girl's face away from her, then grabbed her long hair to keep it there. She lowered her lips to her neck and seemed to bestow a long lasting kiss on her throat. This revived the girl passionately. She writhed and a scream began to emerge from her mouth. This was quickly stopped by the woman, who transferred her lips from throat to mouth and sucked in the agitation of the girl so that she grew as still as death.

Rebecca smirked and withdrew her head lest she be discovered. The sight had been quite heady and exhilarating, reminding her of similar scenes in which she had played a part, though never as a captive. Now, she became aware again of the droning and rapping emerging from beyond the verandah. They would provide further diversion. What other strange sights and experiences might the night hold? she pondered, as she drifted ghostlike towards where the land had been cleared for their new mansion.

Unknown to Rebecca, Amelia had noticed the face at the door, but this had merely increased her pleasure and even her appetite. Reluctantly, she pulled herself away from the supine girl.

'I don't want to take too much from my milch cow,' she said, licking her bloody lips, then bending down again and tonguing away the blood which still dribbled from the two slight punctures. 'We have a long voyage ahead of us and you have to keep up your strength. How did you like my dog? Get off her, you, for she is quite spent, and come close to your mistress.'

George reluctantly disengaged from the girl, whose body lifted slightly from the bed as he withdrew.

'Now, come to me and let me handle you. How strange you natives are down there. There, let Lucy use her tongue. She is not so worn out that she cannot do that. Feel the slit, Lucy. Have you ever felt anything like that before? Your tongue can go right inside it, just as my tongue can go inside you. Now lick me, dog, and hurry. Let us end this night, for tomorrow the ship awaits us and the voyage will be long. If you are good, I shall begin to take some of your blood too. Both of you shall provide me with sustenance, for I have no wish to bring the voyage to an untimely end. Now, savage, enough of your overheated appetite. To your dog shape, and keep this room private with your presence whilst I untie this fair guest and return her to her ungraceful master, nay, I should say husband.'

Amelia untied her captive and helped her up. She went to the door, listened then escorted Lucy through and along the verandah to her own room. Inside, she bandaged the slight wound with a ribbon and then bent and kissed the young woman. 'Sleep well, my child, for there is a long voyage ahead of us on the morrow.'

Now the flat square filled with a crowd of natives standing in solemn rows. They were there to perform the Ghost Dreaming ceremony. Male and female moved towards each other. The men were naked, except for loincloths over which dangled incised pearl shells. The women wore ceremonial grass skirts which left the upper portions of their bodies bare. On their skins they had painted a latticework of white lines which signified a low-cut bodice as in formal European female attire. There was even an appearance of a necklace about their necks with a pedant dangling on their chests. In fact, some had forsaken painting this and wore a piece of cut glass tied on a leather thong. Three white rows of dots were painted on their chests along the cicatrices of womanhood passing across the upper portions of their breasts. Between them, painted in red ochre outlined in white, was an eye shape. To complete their costume, flowers and leafy twigs had been plaited into their hair in an attempt to fashion a European hat.

The men's heads were also ornamented, but with lumps of wood arranged in the shape of top hats or the helmets of soldiers. Their body painting was also inspired from European fashion, both military and civilian. The stripes of military jackets were painted across chests: lapels, collars, pockets and even buttons had been depicted with an attention to detail which might be, and was, startling to eyes other than their own.

Jangamuttuk, Dreamer and owner of the ceremony, wore a real top hat, a beaver somewhat battered, a frockcoat and even trousers, at the crotch of which his pubic shell-covering dangled. Instead of a real waistcoat and stock, he had painted a narrow band of a hatch design about his neck and a spiral design in the vee of the buttoned-up coat.

He sang to his clapsticks, lifting them to his mouth so that the breath of the words might invigorate them. Now he struck them, rap rap-rap, rap rap-rap, and the local didgeridoo players lifted the mouthpiece of their wooden tubes and began to blow out a rhythm which swooped about the steady rap rap-rap, rap rap-rap.

It was not in Sir George's nature to play the sneak unless there was profit to be made from it. He confronted things with a bluster and audacity which often confounded the responses of his critics. Now he wanted to see the corroboree and, by Saint George, he would not only see it but, if his natives objected to his presence, he would order them to continue. Impatiently, he stamped through the garden and was about to make his way through the screen of bush, when he suddenly started back. He had almost stepped on a snake. Unwilling to hazard what else might be there, he went to the track which indirectly gave on to the clearing. He strode along this and smiled when he heard the gruff voice of his old sable friend attempt to mimic the Queen's English in accents not unlike his own.

'They made of me
A ghost down under,
Made for me
A place to plunder,
A place to plunder
Way down under.'

Now the males and females formed couples, clasped each other and began dancing as the rhythm switched to that of a reel. They kept to the repetitive steps and let the rhythm move their feet.

'They made of me
A ghost down under.
Gave me a dram
It tasted like man
Flesh of my flesh,
Real as this dream
Way down under.'

Sir George's eyes adjusted to the soft light from the stars and the sickle moon although it was not bright enough for him to see much detail as he bumbled along. At last the track reached a fork: one prong inclined to the right and went to the harbour, whilst the other went to the left and entered the patch of scrub and trees which, under the stars and moonlight, trembled into a romantic wilderness. The axe had been taken to many of the giant trees to make the track and clear the ground for the foundations. These lay heaved to either side, forming a barricade which cut Sir George off from the corroboree. Perforce, he made his approach along the cart track, which led him to the flickering fires. At the edge of the clearing, a large tree had been left standing and he stood beneath this, watching the natives at their antics.

They were indulging in a ceremony which reminded him of the Mass of the Romish Church. This would not do at the Exhibition and he must make a note of this and adapt it. He observed how the natives divided into couples and approached his old sable friend, Jangamuttuk, who had always been a bit of a rascal and was now acting the part of a priest. Such a wily old savage, one who would bear watching on their trip, for he might take it into his head to go against Sir George's dictates as he had done before. He watched as the old fellow poured into the cupped hands of each couple a liquid of some description which came from a rum bottle.

'What are they doing?' a soft voice asked.

Sir George prided himself as a man without fear. At least, this is how he portrayed his bluster and overbearing manner to himself and to others. In spite of this, he almost jumped a yard into the air before turning to the white shape next to him. Relieved, he recognised the governor's wife. He gave a laugh which was returned. A slender hand came out to touch his side.

'The quaint sounds of these natives roused me from my slumber and, unable to regain my state of repose, I stole forth to observe their ceremonies. Thank God, sir, you are here, for I was ready to take fright as I imagined serpents crawling over my feet. The ceremony appears to be ending and I also became fearful that they might find me, for who knows what nasty things they might do,' Rebecca whispered, shuddering deliciously and also maliciously as the scene of Sir George's wife and a naked savage between her legs came to her.

'These savages are harmless; but still this is not the place for a lady to be,' Sir George observed solemnly. 'Sometimes these ceremonies become indelicate and so, if you allow me, I shall escort you back to the house.'

'Please do,' Rebecca replied, taking his arm and pressing herself against him.

Sir George was taken aback to find that she had no stays on. Always one for the women – and his years had not lessened what he rationalised as a natural need – he still felt somewhat reluctant to acknowledge the response of his body to the soft pressure against his side. To cover his sudden arousal, he huffed and puffed and drew away from the contact.

They regained the track and soon left the shelter of the wood to come under the light of the stars and moon. He stopped and glanced back, then down at the woman whose nightdress seemed to glow, though her body appeared as shadows under the cloth. The light was kind to her face, smoothing out the wrinkles so that he had to recall her age and wastage. Still, he was not adverse to mature women, especially when his wife was young and innocent and he hesitated to practise with her the little distractions he had learnt to appreciate during his eventful life.

'The night is so beautiful, so delicate and pleasant, and I am not the least sleepy,' the woman murmured at his side. 'Perhaps we can stay out a little longer,' she added with a little laugh and a glance whose import was lost in the gloom.

Sir George acquiesced and they walked around the dilapidated garden to where they could obtain a view of the harbour. Out on the water lay the long bulk of the *Great Britain*, lamps gleaming in her five masts and along her monstrous length.

Amelia had slipped from Lucy's room and was closing the door when a dark figure appeared at her side. It said: 'Well, when the master is away the slaves and women will play. What have you been up to?'

'Taking my sustenance, John – or should that be Wadawaka?' Amelia replied gaily, going to the African and wrapping her arms about him. 'And where have you been? What is that paint on you?'

'John or Wadawaka, one or the other will do. I have just come back from the ceremony. Once, they had the power to move me; now the magic is gone. The time upon the whaler has coarsened my sensibilities and, well, to lose a battle is not to my liking.' Saying this, he bent and kissed her lightly on the lips to make peace between them, then he drew back having tasted her repast. 'There is blood on your lips, as they have blood on their hands.'

'What, do you expect me to starve? But this night no one has died. I lick it away. Now, they are – well, no matter, look at the night and how the stars beckon. There is magic in the air and the melodies of your fellows sound romantic from the distance. Let us take to the air and enjoy the freedom of the sky. Skimming over this dark land will be our way of saying farewell. Such adventures you and I have had here where we first met, separated and came together again. As I've said, the night makes me romantic and thus I forget for a time what you did to me.'

And with this, her pale form shimmered, dissolved in the starlight and reformed into the dark shape of a bat which flickered up into the air. Wadawaka watched her for a moment before he too vanished to reform in a camouflage of spotted fur that merged with the soft shadows of the moon and stars.

Leopard gave a snarl and took to the air, speeding after the bat who began flickering around him in sudden swoops and dives. He paddled with his paws, seeking to catch her, but managed only to disrupt the smoothness of his flight. She flashed along his belly between his legs, then swung about his tail and landed on his back. He growled as he felt her claws rip through his skin and into his flesh. She drooped her wings and rested there as he turned and sped towards the sea. He reached the quay, where the lanterns of soldiers guarded the shoreline to prevent sailors from deserting their ships and joining the gold rush, then flew low over the water and along the enormous length of the *Great Britain*.

'Such a massive piece of iron,' Amelia said in his mind. 'Isn't it magical that such a mass of iron can float on the water? One would think that it would sink.'

'It is as great and as oppressive as the empire that built it,' Leopard replied. 'No natural thing can match it and even Moby Dick is just a minnow beside it. What are our magical stories compared to its solid reality?'

'You and your whales and sea things. Enough of this floating lump of iron which lacks a magician's touch. A mountain range is bigger and more majestic and holds greater secrets within its bowels,' and she released her hold and fluttered down, a tiny black glove drifting about the five masts as if to defy their massiveness with her slightness. She might have even landed on the deck, but Leopard came after her and Bat left off any designs she might have had and darted towards the shore with him in pursuit. He had almost reached her when she closed her wings and dropped down among the thick boles of trees. She entwined herself among the branches while Leopard, owing to his bulk, stayed at tree-top level.

Others were also regarding the ship. Rebecca stared at it and suddenly gave a shudder. 'It seems, it seems like a huge serpent resting on the waters. It would be a little scary, but you are soon to shelter in her womb,' she murmured, touching the knight lightly on the shoulder and leaving her hand there. Sir George himself was quite overcome by the huge vessel; for him, the massy bulk signified the future. He examined the long length of iron with a proprietary interest.

'It is more than leviathan,' he declared. 'The natives talk of giant serpents, but we in our conquest of the elements manufacture them. This indeed is the age of greatness and soon there will be larger ships afloat, even though the mind boggles to contemplate them. That vessel is over three hundred and fifty feet long and fifty wide. A true example of our empire, the greatest the world has ever seen. Perhaps in honour of our age, and if you can get the governor to forward the proposal to the colonial office, this colony so vast in extent could be renamed Great Westland, and this town – which one day will be a gigantic city with factories and dwellings covering the surrounding hills – could be called Albert, after the Prince Consort.'

'I too admire things great,' Rebecca said, snuggling up against the older man. She stared at the ship and suddenly recalled her plan. She wanted to be on her, leaving this forsaken land. It was time for her to make her move.

'Call me Rebecca – no, use my pet name, Becky,' she murmured. 'Indeed, this is a vast ship with room for hundreds, though it will leave here almost empty. I would like to be on her on what will be an historic voyage, for she is certain to create a record. The captain at dinner was insistent on her ability.'

'We all would like to be on her and tomorrow –'

'Which reminds me. The governor has reconsidered your land grant and has decided that I should participate in the mission that will do so much to alleviate the plight of the wild inhabitants of this land.'

'What, what?' the knight almost shouted in his consternation. 'The governor assured me that the grant would go through as the Deed was drafted. It will set back my plans if the ownership is divided, and harm the raising of capital.'

'My husband may appear lacking, but he is always on the lookout for his benefit. If the Deed of Grant were in his own name, he would interfere constantly and it is only because I thought of you that I urged this course,' Becky replied, then added: 'We are partners, and as partners we should be on our guard against such schemes as my husband may initiate. It will be to both our benefits that I travel with you to the metropolis where I can contact Lord Steyne who, I know, will be very interested in this colony now that copious amounts of gold have been discovered. I must go and I will go. A mother cannot be separated from her son. It is too cruel.' And she began sobbing, pressing her little wilted face against his shoulder. 'Please, please,' she begged him. 'Please, please,' she implored, holding onto his arm tightly. 'Sway my husband to let me go, for he respects you and will heed your words, unlike mine, for he is a tyrant where women are concerned. You are the leader of our projected greatness and must put my case to him. Please,' she urged, then added coquettishly: 'Pretty please, and I will be grateful to you and will show it to you in ways which a man of the world might appreciate.'

'Well, well,' Sir George replied, put out by what the governor had done to him, and turning vindictive at the duplicity. 'Well,' he said again, whilst thinking that the fellow had broken his word and thus his honour. He could have no compunction now in furthering his own interests and getting this woman on side. 'Well,' he said again and found a weapon in subterfuge. 'It might be better if the governor shared the grant with me and could accompany me to London. Well, it can't be helped and indeed might be for the better. We have a queen, and a woman with the right connections might even gain her ear or that of her consort whom you have met; and Lord Steyne, although well along in years, is not to be dismissed. The Prince Consort holds him in good regard, as you doubtless know.'

'You will not regret putting yourself out to further my small case. A woman is always guided by her needs and desires. I must see my son,' Becky maintained stoutly, though she had shown little grief when she put him into boarding school, and had written only a few letters since she had been in the colony. Still, she mimed wiping away a tear, before changing the topic. 'I feel a sudden chill,' she declared, embracing her partner, half turning so that her breasts flattened against him. She smiled as she felt his breath increase, and the scene of his wife and that savage re-entered her mind to quicken her own breath. Free from her stays, her body felt ready to turn this old fellow to her advantage.

'In Paris, I was wined and feted and even met the then king,' she murmured. 'The Frenchmen were so charming with pretty habits that they liked satisfied. A woman my age is so much better attuned to a man's needs than a ninny like your wife. I have eaten such for breakfast, but she is a pretty little thing and suits you well. In your travels, have you been to Paris and perhaps had a dainty coquette with an interesting mouth? They are quite adept at what is called, with good reason, French kissing.'

Sir George's breath got the better of his voice. He knew of the reputation this woman had and indeed it made her exciting.

Amelia came across the entwined figures and flickered about them. The woman squealed and held on more tightly to the man. Bat gleefully flapped at their heads, then settled in a tree to watch the fun; but from above came a growl from Leopard and she fluttered away to him.

'More victims!' he spoke in her head.

'No, two rogues that deserve each other,' she replied in the same manner. 'But enough of them, let us make for that hill which overlooks the town and harbour.'

Bat flicked Leopard's nose in passing as she sped off. By the time he had caught up, the bat had been replaced by the human. As he landed, she ran to him, her fingers talons to rake through his fur. She gripped him hard, feeling the electric transference of atoms as he changed into a man. The current made her gasp. She rested against his broad chest for a moment, before drawing back, though keeping hold of his hand; or rather, his hand encased her own and she allowed it to remain captured.

They stood side by side, staring down at the town and the length of the ship glowing at anchor, a long line of promised progress with which, in time, they would have to deal. Both thought the same thought, for as one they turned and stared inland where darkness reigned and nothing appeared to move. Peace and quiet stretched before them and over it they could fly without the need for evasion.

'I might miss this land,' Amelia said softly. 'It is strange that I came here as a thing limited to my own patch of earth and the darkness of the night. Within her, I gained the power to face the burning blast of the day and freedom from the tyranny of the sun. I was reborn in her depths and will miss her.'

'She did not bring as much to me as she did to you, for I am of the ocean and the land lacks the hidden currents and constant movements that move my soul. Why I became Leopard I do not know, for I should have been a sea creature, perhaps that Moby Dick, and battled those puny land creatures which came against me.'

'Too much sea in you for my thirst,' she replied with a laugh, then added: 'You do not like this place because I trapped you underground and made you mine. Well, you wanted me as much as I wanted you; how else could such a powerful animal as Leopard allow himself to be trapped by the black glove of a bat?'

She turned to him and wrapped her arms about him. She was a pale streak of loveliness across the dark length of his body, seemingly embedded in it as a streak of silver ore. She writhed against him, caressing him with her whole body as she drifted around to his back. Now only her two silver arms could be seen from the front. 'Not much of softness here,' she exclaimed. 'How could such as I imprison you with these thin bonds? The softness is in your mind and that is what appeals to me.'

'The whip hardens the body, but stripes the mind,' the man said bitterly. 'To have been a slave is to be maimed.'

'Well, well, well, I'm as much a slave to you as you are to me, for we own each other,' she replied, laughing again. She found where the bat's claws had pierced his skin and drawn blood. Without extending her fangs, she put forth her tongue and gently lapped up the few bitter drops. She almost gagged, but continued on, until his shoulders suddenly quivered in response to her fangs gently slipping into his skin.

'Don't worry, your blood is as sea water to a thirsty man. Still, I am sure that if I believed in slavery, I might make you one; but it is not even a joke to indulge in. Forgive me. We are both free spirits and refuse to accept the ownership of others.'

'Yes, we have our liberty, though where we are going I will be below the white, and in other places my freedom would be a matter of documents. I have been owned and that is an experience not to be borne.'

'No thoughts of what is past and what you have suffered. We are above them and their attempts to hurt. In your darkness, I find myself and, and —'

'In your whiteness, I tremble, knowing you for what you are,' he replied.

'Do so, for I have not forgiven you,' Amelia rejoined tartly. 'Now, the night is passing and the land flows over us in all its glory. Let us return to my chamber so that I might make you tremble in another and more satisfying way.'

Her pale loveliness lost its shapeliness and transformed into an ugly bat which took to the air gracefully. The man's dark bulk resumed a shape which was powerful and a thing of beauty. Leopard allowed Bat to settle on his back and he slowly carried her towards the dwelling. The stars hung overhead and the sickle moon shone down on their contentment. They passed over the deserted clearing where the fires had died down to glowing beds of coals, and were close to the house when they noticed an indistinct patch of whiteness quaking below them. They descended lower and saw that it was Sir George and the governor's wife, who was manipulating his body. They heard his sudden gasp followed by a shuddering moan which abruptly cut off as voices sounded. Then Leopard carried Bat away from the sight and to the verandah of the house where they transformed into their human shapes and, still clinging together so that they had to manoeuvre their united bulk through the narrow doorway, entered.

Dog came out to settle himself down on the verandah. He pricked up his ears as Rebecca hastened past him, then growled as Sir George followed. Now all was quiet and he curled himself into a ball and drifted away into thoughts of the earth smelling sweetly in his nostrils and the scent of his prey rising to beckon him on.

Sir George, to tell the truth, was more overcome by the vessel before him than the woman beside him. It was up to Becky to initiate the action and she did so without modesty. Her small hand reached out to touch the front of his trousers. She rubbed her thumb up and down.

The knight rose to the occasion physically, but there was still some doubt in his mind about taking liberties with the woman, even if she was ready for them. So, it was true that she had sullied her reputation in England.

Becky had been deprived of variety and domination for too long and now, as her fingers freed him, she began her conquest. She sank to her knees and her dainty mouth began to work on him, so much so that he could hardly think and the lights and shape of the huge ship did appear to be a leviathan with its mouth at his loins. It abruptly withdrew. His hands went to her head to push her lips back on him; but she got to her feet and turned her back to him with a gesture which spurred him on. The little minx, she knew what he liked. He lifted her chemise and thrust forward.

'Great, great,' he groaned, his eyes clinging to the long length of the ship. He imagined the bows slicing through the waters and plunging deep within the waves. 'All iron, all hard as iron and over three hundred and fifty feet in length,' he moaned, plunging hard into her.

'Deeper, deeper,' Becky moaned in unison, bent over and staring at the ship, imagining herself in one of the staterooms. 'So nice, it will be so nice,' she whispered, pushing back against his thrusts.

Sir George's hands went around her breasts and he held on as he worked away in a frenzy. The goal was in sight and his mind seemed to splinter so that the lights of the ship multiplied and the hills glowed, glittering with the covering of a vast city. Machines pounded away and countless vehicles thrust through the streets. He felt himself on the verge of spending his all in a great rush when Becky, perfectly under control, fell away and to the ground. He followed, anxious for his fulfilment, but she evaded his attempts and said, coldly, before recollecting herself and seeking for a warmer tone: 'There'll be time for this on that ship and we can have our full of each other in comfort. Promise me that you'll be accommodated next to me. Promise me that,' she urged, reaching out and squeezing his penis.

'Yes, yes, you are necessary for our great project,' he moaned. He would have promised anything by now, and she knew it.

'And then you'll have all of me, and perhaps some more,' she said with a cruel laugh, for soon this place would be of the past and she would re-enter her old circles. She imagined relating this episode to Lord Steyne, who liked to hear such things. 'But as a future promise, I'll do this,' she added, moving her hand up and down until Sir George suddenly jerked and went limp.

Becky got to her feet and stared down in triumph at the old fool. 'Next time, it'll be far, far better,' she said in a soft voice. Suddenly she gave a start as she felt the presence of others nearby. Once, she had been caught in similar circumstances and it still rankled. How could she have been so stupid? But this time the only observers were three natives. They stood there motionless. Unfrazzled, and without a backward glance at the man on the ground, she walked off towards her waiting bed and sleeping husband. She did not even try to make out the words of the voice of one of the natives.

'Fada, you still up to your tricks. But watch that one; she is just as bad as that Amelia. Keep that thing covered and for your wife.'

'Yeah, you should do that, Fada,' Jangamuttuk added to the words of his wife. 'Remember how you taught us to sing "How Great Thou Art"? Well, it may be true for Hercules here, but not for you. Look at that shrivelled little thing now. Not as long and as hard as that iron ship there.'

Laughing, they walked off, leaving the gasping and embarrassed Sir George to get to his feet.

When he returned to his room, he stared down at his young and innocent wife as she lay calmly sleeping. He wondered what simple dreams roamed about in her head. He bent closer to examine the ribbon about her neck. The poor thing must have injured herself for there were spots of blood on it. His mind returned to the scene of his recent encounter and he felt himself rising again. He went to the wash stand, poured some water, lifted his nightdress and washed himself, then sank into the bed. He was weary, but large with expectation. How great thou art indeed, he smiled as he slipped into his wife, thinking of Becky. The massive vessel came into his mind just as he spent himself. 'Such greatness,' he murmured, as he rolled away from his sleeping wife. Soon, his snores arose.

Such were the actions of those who, on the morrow, would be leaving the dismal colony.

EXTRACT FROM
HER MAJESTY'S DIARY

May 8. Went to the Exhibition where we remained for two hours. What held my attention and amazed me was the Great Westland Exhibition. The well-known native pacifist, Sir George Augustus, together with his lady wife, Lucille, and Rebecca Crawley, the spouse of the governor of the said colony, and the mysterious and heavily veiled Amelia Fraser, whose sketches of scenes from the colony were on display, were there in attendance. I have invited the governor's lady and Amelia Fraser to take tea with me at the palace. Both seem strong-willed women of the empire. Under the supervision of Sir George was a group of the native inhabitants who, although the exhibition was really for the inanimate products of the land, put on a lively show for us. What is called a corroboree, I believe. I was startled to see how the natives mimicked some of the aspects of our customs. Sir George explained that this revealed that the process of civilising such creatures was well underway. What struck my fancy was a singular instrument of wood, a simple tube from which the blower extracted a number of sounds, even to that of a bugle call. I accepted one of these as a gift from an old man, who seemed to be their chief, and also a tapestry of that savage land so unique.

I was quite taken with the performance, but what was really striking and an object which bodes well for the future of the colony, was a gigantic nugget or slug of gold of some pounds in weight, which nature had marvellously fashioned in the shape of a golden fleece. This was the central piece of the exhibition and I was informed that it has caused much comment in the city, as well as being one of the premier attractions. In fact, my dear Albert was so impressed with it that he confided to Lord Steyne, who was one of the party, that he wished he might visit the colony as it was on the edge of my far-flung possessions and indeed needed, with the advent of the discovery of gold and exploitation of the same, to be brought closer to the centre, as it were. I hope that my dear husband will not undertake such a long trip, as the thought of being separated from him for some months is not to be borne. Such were my tender feelings on the subject that I felt quite done and exhausted. We left at a quarter to twelve.